SHTETL ON THE GRAND

Gerald Tulchinsky

DEDICATION

To the memory of Herman Fawcett,
history teacher extraordinaire

 FriesenPress

Suite 300 - 990 Fort St
Victoria, BC, Canada, V8V 3K2
www.friesenpress.com

ISBN
978-1-4602-5954-2 (Hardcover)
978-1-4602-5955-9 (Paperback)
978-1-4602-5956-6 (eBook)

1. Fiction, Cultural Heritage

Distributed to the trade by The Ingram Book Company

TABLE OF CONTENTS

PREFACE

I'm from Brantford, what I call a "shtetl on the Grand," the Jewish small community on the Grand River in Western Ontario. I was born there in September 1933 and spent my early years with parents, two sisters, and a brother living in rented houses located mainly in the rough end of Eagle Place, an industrial section of town. Our house on Greenwich Street was sandwiched between an active railway spur line at the rear and a foul-smelling canal in front. The railway boxcars housed the sad men, called "hoboes," who begged for food from households, including ours, along the line. I shall never forget them. Many ended their stay in Brantford at the end of this spur line, in the "Jungle," a wooded area located down past the glue factory. The canal ran into the Grand River, whose fertile lands had been granted to the Six Nations Iroquois by the British in 1784.

I attended King Edward Public School and, when we moved to Dundas Street up on Terrace Hill, I was a pupil at Graham Bell Public School, and then at the Brantford Collegiate Institute and Vocational School.

From almost earliest memory, I was made aware that I was a Jew and was therefore basically different from other kids in these neighbourhoods. At the age of six I was taken aside roughly and told by a local woman who lived next to Mrs. Pickering's candy store: "You are a Jew and you don't belong here. This is not your country." (Full disclosure: I was the youngest and smallest member of a gang of neighbourhood boys who stole pears off her backyard tree, and I couldn't escape over the fence in time.)

"You are a Jew and you don't belong here. This is not your country." This is not an assertion one forgets, although it took me quite a few years to absorb its poisonous meaning.

Reinforcement of this message came in the form of periodic violence, frequent name-calling and fistfights that reminded me, my siblings, and other Jews that we were some kind of enemy. One of the most frequent taunts was: "You killed Jesus!" to which one wag responded: "But why didn't you stop me?"

Still, I didn't need these experiences to know that Jews were different. From the kosher food we ate to my family's strong Zionist affiliation, we were conscious and enormously proud of who we were. What was less easy to absorb was the concept that Jews didn't belong in Canada.

These stories are fictional but loosely based on some of the experiences I had growing up in Brantford, with a consciousness of a special identity reinforced by a Jewish community made up mostly of East European immigrants who had arrived before the First World War, or the Great War, as it was then called. This collection is not an autobiography, but I am in there somewhere.

I wrote these stories over recent years and showed them to colleagues and friends, including Jack Granatstein and Mel Wiebe, who have made many excellent suggestions and provided very strong encouragement, especially when energies flagged. And I owe a great debt to Jim Pritchard, Jacalyn Duffin, May Polsky, Zev Klein, Ted Tulchinsky (my brother), Hilary and Peter Neary (who suggested this title), and Patricia Robertson, who read all or some of them and offered very useful suggestions. Stuart Woolley helped me sort out a couple of endings. Michel Pharand revised the final draft and made many valuable corrections and suggestions. My wife, Ruth, read everything critically and eventually lovingly approved.

Although I have translated some Yiddish and Hebrew words and expressions in parentheses in the text, readers may also want to consult the Glossary, at the end of this book, for further definitions and explanations.

GREENHORN

"How much money do you want?"

Roderick MacKinnon, the manager of the Brantford branch of the Bank of Nova Scotia, was addressing Yankel Bucavetsky, who sat across from him, his massive hands resting squarely on the old oak desk.

"How much," Yankel replied in a flash, "have you got?"

MacKinnon stared at him for a moment, then exploded in laughter.

As a newcomer to town a day earlier, Yankel, a burly man of just over medium height, had walked from the CNR station to see a "landsman" (a fellow townsman) whom his family in Tiraspol, Bessarabia—now in independent Moldavia—knew lived in Brantford. This was Hesh Murafsky, who, in this year of 1926, was the proud proprietor of a grocery store in the Albion Street neighbourhood that embraced the shul and about two dozen Jewish families living undisturbed in the midst of a large population of recent Armenian, Hungarian, Italian, Polish, and Ukrainian immigrants, and their churches and meeting halls (both anti- and pro-communist.)

Murafsky had settled there in 1910 and, in his capacity as chief grocer to the inhabitants of the city's multi-ethnic ghetto, lived at the crossroads of what academic social scientists would later pompously call "information flows." In his store and on the street Murafsky was consulted by customers and neighbours for news and gossip on current local politics, on the state of marital or extramarital liaisons, on the chastity of the young women, on the gambling debts of the "boys" who gathered for poker on Sunday afternoons in his dining room behind the store, and—for business!

Not the price of Canadian Pacific Railway shares on the Toronto Stock Exchange or the current balance of trade between Canada and Great Britain, and certainly not the facts and figures gathered by the local Chamber of Commerce. To Murafsky, business meant the markup on dresses in Kivenko's "Fashion Lane," or the wholesale price of the sofas in "Renkle's Home Furnishings" and suspenders at "Tabby's Men's Clothing," or the comparative quality of merchandise at other Jewish establishments in the city's downtown Colborne/Dalhousie/Market Street nexus. He knew, or said he knew, the daily price—even hourly variations—of scrap iron and other recyclables, mainly metals paid by Hamilton brokers to the dozen or so local Jews who scoured the town and nearby rural areas for this "junk," stored it in their yards (located mostly down by the CNR repair shops) and waited for upswings in demand. He was even up to date on the asking and selling prices of the humble houses in the neighbourhood.

Heaven knows how Murafsky received such information. Perhaps it came on the wind, blowing through his rattly windows and gusting through the busy door of his emporium. Maybe he learned of these things by sniffing the outside air or eating the briny pickles and herring from the barrels in his basement. Certainly it was true that information, misinformation, rumours, lies, slander, and gossip of all kinds, came to this wispy little man and his gargantuan wife in such quantity and diversity that it was mostly beyond him. In any case, as he depended on neighbourhood good will, he let it be known that he deliberately forgot most of what he heard. And although no one believed him, he was sought after by many who believed that he had it all at his fingertips, Jewish guys drifting into town from God-knows-where: recently-arrived immigrants, con men, schnorrers, itinerant teachers and rabbis collecting money for yeshivas in Europe or the Holy Land, various salesmen, all the here-today-gone-tomorrow people, gathered like moths to light at Murafsky's emporium to seek his advice and to give him news and impressions of the outside world—and perhaps to "borrow" a few dollars to have a little something to eat.

And full of stories they were, sitting around in his store filled with everything from pickles to peanuts that the neighbourhood housewives could afford for their kitchen tables. The drifters told all kinds of stories, about life in their home town or "der alter heim" (the old home), their families, old loves, former neigh-bours, wives and children left behind, famous rabbis, and life as conscripts in the army of Czar Nikolai, "zoll er brennen" (may he burn in Hell), they usually added. Stories about departures and arrivals: pogroms, the quest for the right papers, elusive passports, visas, police clearances, jail time, detentions, health inspections, and other procedures they had endured before boarding ship. And their voyages to Canada. Stories to make you howl with rage, dance with joy, cry with pain, and laugh with love or hate.

All of this attention made Murafsky an important man in town; he was the person to consult, to advise, to show, to pair off buyers and sellers—he was even asked to make marriage arrangements—and to adjudicate disputes. And did he act the part! He always sat at the front of the synagogue (known to all Jews as the shul), smiling benignly at members of the congregation; he gave to chari-ties, extended small personal loans at no interest, was an honoured guest at Armenian, Hungarian, Italian, Polish, and Ukrainian celebrations, and he bid generously for honours in the shul—all of which he gave away to others. He enjoyed being the centre of attention as the community's leading man, next only to old Rabbi Yacobovsky, of course.

Yankel Bucavetsky had arrived in Halifax two years before aboard the S.S. *Madonna* along with nearly 500 other young Jewish refugees living in Romania, refugees from the Russian civil war and ensuing pogroms. After a two-day train trip to Toronto, he'd drifted in and out of various low-end jobs—who would hire a greenhorn for anything else?—and, to make a long story short, ended up in town because of – who knows? – the price of the train ticket, the search for his landsman, a rumour about jobs, advice from a supposed maven (an expert), or just plain luck.

"Fun vanen kumt a Yid?" (Where does a Jew come from?) Murafsky was speaking Yiddish to Yankel, who had just entered the store carrying his roped-up cardboard suitcase.

"Tiraspol."

"Tiraaaspoolll, Tiraspol, Tiraspol. TIRASPOL," shouted Murafsky who then launched into a croaky version of one of the risqué verses of the popular song "Roumania, Roumania."

"And what brought you here?" he said, ending his shtick abruptly as his wife entered the store from their living quarters behind.

"I'm looking around."

"For what?"

"Parnosa."

"Oh parnosa! He's looking to make a living here." This was said to no one in particular, but it looked as if Murafsky was addressing the rack of men's workshirts off to the right.

"Who isn't, shmendrik?" Murafsky loved to tease greenhorns with such words suggesting he was speaking to a dope.

Yankel took a firm step forward, set his blue eyes on Murafsky, and said nothing. Then slowly, "I'm thinking about the junk business."

"Junk? He's thinking about the junk business." Murafsky informed the wall of canned peas, carrots, and a vast assortment of jams and spreads.

"What do you know about junk?"

"What's to know?" said Yankel. "You buy cheap and sell dear."

"Listen to him," Murafsky chortled, waving to the ceiling. "'Buy cheap and sell dear'," he says. "Buy from who and sell to who?"

"From the train I saw lots of scrap metal lying around outside the factories. That's where I'll buy. In Hamilton they make steel. That's where I'll sell. I want to buy a truck and rent a yard."

"Oy, this greener is so smaaaart," intoned Murafsky. "And where will you get capital, my greener?" he said, looking at Yankel's old suitcase.

"I got twenty-six dollars."

Murafsky started to dance, singing the old synagogue tune of "L'cho Dodi": "He's got twenty-six dollars to buy some junk. He's got twenty-six dollars to buy some junk." … "You're serious?"

"Yes."

"You're serious?"

"Nu, what else?"

"OK, landsman. Let me give you some advice. You need capital, and in Canada we get capital from banks." Murafsky's chest had enlarged.

"A bank?"

"Yes, a bank! Oy, what a greener!" he informed the sacks of flour on the floor in front of the counter.

"Where's a bank?"

"In town there are banks. I know where they are."

"You know where they are? You can show me?"

"I can show you. In fact, me and my bank manager, Mister Roderick A. MacKinnon, are just like that." Murafsky put two fingers together and stuck them under Yankel's nose.

"Just like that?"

"He's my friend. I'll take you to him. Don't worry. I'll translate for you. I know English."

The next day Murafsky, dressed in his best suit, accompanied Yankel down to the Bank of Nova Scotia and entered MacKinnon's glassed-in office.

"Mister MacKinnon," said Murafsky.

"Mister …" he hesitated. "Mister … aaa—"

"Murafsky, you know, the grocer."

"Ohhh yes, of course. How are you? And what can I—"

"This is Yankel Bucavetsky. He came recently from the old country. I am giving him advice and he wants a loan to go in the junk business. I'll have to translate for him."

MacKinnon nodded and then fixed his eyes squarely on Yankel for several long seconds. The banker knew the ins and outs of junk, having already backed the buoyant Melzers, Revzenskys, and Ravnitskys in the business over recent years. He continued to look intently across his desk, though Yankel's "How much have you got?" had left him smiling.

"What's it for, Mr. Bucavetsky?"

"For buy truck, one hundred dollars, Mister."

"You wish to go into the junk business?"

"Yes, Mister."

"Where?"

"Here. Right in Brantford. I got twenty-six dollars, Mister." Yankel, with his massive hands, had twisted his cap into several shapes.

MacKinnon studied Yankel, then scribbled some figures on his desk pad.

"You have twenty-six dollars and you want to buy a truck for one hundred dollars. That means you need seventy-four dollars."

"Sure, and then I buy junk for cost maybe fifty dollars. And then I get yard for cost fifty dollars one year. Listen Mister, I make good business. I need two hundred dollars. Can pay you fast back again."

MacKinnon sat back in his chair, then said: "How old are you?"

"Thirty-four years, Mister. I got a family, wife and little boy."

"What do you know about junk?"

"I work two years by Frenkel, you know, the big junk dealer in Toronto."

"How much do they pay in Hamilton for scrap iron these days?"

"Yesterday was price four dollars sixty cents each ton."

MacKinnon opened a drawer and glanced inside. He looked over at Yankel's face and big hands.

"Where will you rent a yard?"

"Over by railway. I already found one place, by Peruniak, Grand Trunk Street. Fifty dollars for year."

"Well…"

"I work hard, Mister. I pay you back. Don't worry nothings. I work hard."

Silence.

MacKinnon nodded slowly and said "Ooookay, Mister Bucavetsky. I'll extend you a line of credit for one year for two hundred dollars at three percent interest. We'll open an account for you and I expect you to make payments every month. Good luck."

He stood up, smiled and held out his hand. "Thank you, gentlemen."

"You see," said Murafsky, as they walked out. "In this country you got to know the right people. Connections count for everything. Like I told you: me and the bank manager are just like *that*! And I'm glad I could translate for you."

"Sure, Hesh," nodded Yankel, smiling ruefully to himself. "Sure."

"JEW! YOU CANNOT LIVE HERE."

This warning was splashed in large black letters on the living-room wall in early October 1938 at Brantford's 207 Terrace Hill Street, the two-storey house that David Stemeroff, "Zaida" to his family, had just bought. (The incident occurred within a month of Germany's Kristallnacht, which some historians consider the beginning of the Holocaust.) The family hadn't moved in yet and the perps must have entered through an unlocked door or window.

Family members quickly painted the wall, but it was defaced again in the same way and several windows were smashed a day or so later. So when they did occupy their "new" house, they were well aware of the deep hostility that surrounded them. News from Europe was also frightening, though, of course, they knew full well that Brantford was not Berlin. Still, local antisemitism was familiar to them: there was plenty of it around. Jobs were scarce. Schoolyard taunts and fights in parks and neighbourhood streets let Jewish kids know that they were not the equals of the MacGregors and the Joneses. "You killed Jesus!" one kid on his way home from Sunday School shouted at them. "No I didn't," Buntsy Walzer retorted, "but maybe Mrs. Steinberg did."

Jews were not allowed to join the service organizations, and the Golf and Country Club was strictly off-limits, even for vets like Albert Cohen, who had joined the family dry goods business on returning from the Great War with only one arm and a metal plate in his skull after being wounded at Passchendaele.

Sometimes there was revenge, as attested by the famous reaction of four local Jewish boys who set upon the Collegiate's physics teacher for repeatedly slapping around little Jack Cohen. And the then-legendary Billy Bucavetsky's prowess in all team sports and at fisticuff encounters injected a good measure of pride. However soothed by these triumphs, the community of storekeepers and junk dealers and their families generally preferred to keep quiet so as not to arouse controversy and possibly fuel more antisemitism.

And this practice was confirmed at the hastily summoned conference of self-appointed community worthies held in the large booth at the rear of Greco's Grill, the downtown hangout of the Colborne Street Jewish shopkeepers, to discuss the Terrace Hill incident. Furniture store owner and long-time Brantfordite, Louis Renkle, presided. A big Bavarian who had been a cop on New York's Lower East Side before migrating north, he had some understanding of power and its limitations, and, as a self-appointed representative of the German enlightenment, he had awarded himself pride of place over the other local Jews, most of whom hailed from the backwaters of Eastern Europe. Alongside him sat Sam Nyman, a thin chain-smoker and migrant from Poland, whose large shop featuring classy women's fashions dominated the street. The third member was Isaac Ravnitsky, a burly junk dealer from Bessarabia with a vast yard on Grand Trunk Street, who collected scrap metal from local metal-working factories and numerous machine shops; he sent truckloads twice-weekly to the Hamilton dealers supplying the giant furnaces at Stelco and Dofasco.

Cokes in place, the conference began with Renkle's usual references to "the law and constitution," a phrase he regularly employed to overwhelm and intimidate the locals because it implied superior knowledge and conjured up in their minds Czarist oppression they preferred to forget. He then loudly stated the options before the community in the wake of the recent events at the Stemeroffs.

Call the police? "Never!!" cried Ravnitsky, who had experienced beatings on the soles of his feet during police interrogations in his native land and viewed all cops as corrupt brutes—and antisemites to a man.

Call City Hall? Nyman noted that Mayor Sam MacBride was a thoroughly decent man, but that his dramatic seizure of several tons of coal at the CNR yards for the shivering poor last winter had aroused fear of "Bolshevism" and deep resentment in the upscale West End. Alderman John Patrick Ryan, a printer and most admirable man, had expressed sympathy and introduced a motion in city council roundly condemning the violence and urging a vigorous police investigation. But why link the Jews to such controversial figures—who could do nothing anyway?

Call the Congress? The Canadian Jewish Congress was the "voice of our people," but, as Renkle complained, except for fussing around at their Montreal and Toronto offices, the pompous bigwigs could do nothing much and would probably stir up other issues that were of no consequence to Brantford's Jews.

Call the newspaper? *The Expositor* was known to local wags as "The Suppository." Owner Cornelius Throckmorton Weston, a patrician and distant figure with a grand house on tony Dufferin Avenue, was a man not known for harbouring sympathy for the common herd—especially not for recent immigrants. The city's working-class Armenians, Chinese, Hungarians, Italians, Negroes, Poles, and Ukrainians could expect little from this quarter. And as a leading Protestant churchman and Grand Master of the local Orange Lodge, he had no truck with the Irish Catholics in town. As for the Jews? Don't ask!

To come right down to it, what could *anybody* do? The conferees agreed that, regrettably, such was the case. So, after exchanging some minor community gossip and lamentations over the intensity of the new rabbi's religious fervour, they shook hands and left the restaurant.

Stemeroff, for his part, thought things over as the family moved in after decorating all of the rooms and painting the outside wood a bright shade of green. He thought about the ugly events as he tried to get acquainted with the neighbours, all of them staying stony-faced while he tintroduced himself: "Hallow. Mine nam iz Shteymirow, Daweed Shteymirow." But often he never got that far because the door would be slammed in his face while he proudly stated "Hallow. Mine na—."

He would then retreat to his own property. Winter came and he shoveled his walkway and the front sidewalk. In the spring he mowed his front lawn and planted flowers up against the house and at several places across the lawn. In his large back yard he dug up the soil and planted beds of vegetables: several varieties of tomatoes, carrots, lettuce, radishes, green and Spanish onions, red and green peppers, string and wax beans, and potatoes, plus a patch of dill. And flowers between those groups and around the edge of the entire garden.

He brought in apple, plum, pear, and cherry trees and planted them throughout. He built a chicken coop for laying hens and ducks. In his workshop he built and painted little wooden benches and chairs of different designs and scattered them throughout the garden—he pronounced it "gardain"—and he would sit out there in good weather smoking his handmade fags. He weeded by hand and hoed his patches daily. He spent so much time out there that he seemed to be at one with his plants, occasionally lifting his head over them and turning his face upward to the sun.

In late summer his harvest was immense. Produce came in by the bushelfull. The family canned much of it; jams and relishes were cooked and vats of pickles were put down for future use. But he set aside the best of his harvest for something special: gifts for his neighbours. He took his produce around in cardboard boxes to their front doors, knocked or rang the bell. But the doors never opened, so he sighed and left his vegetables and fruits on the porches.

These offerings, then, made no difference, and the family continued to live in isolation, the neighbours shunning them as undesirable aliens. Over the years, if they happened to pass each other on the sidewalk, the Bennetts and the MacGregors continued to turn their faces away when Stemeroff said "Hallow."

Maybe it was his appearance that continued to put them off. Not only was Stemeroff a Jew; he was, after all, a junk peddler whose collections around the streets by horse and wagon were a familiar, but unwelcome, sight.

The wagon had seen rough service and the horse was a worn-out, grey beast called "Nudnik" who needed constant encouragement. And his loading and unloading of scrap metal, bottles, rags, paper, hides, and other detritus did nothing to enhance the look of his wardrobe, especially his long black coat, which featured prominent tears and stains. After a day of such collecting, he transported his junk to a barn—he pronounced it "barrrenn"—that he rented in the neighbourhood.

His work hat, not his snappy Sabbath and Liberal Party meeting fedora, was an ancient, overlarge, brownish trilby that had long ago lost its original colour, shape, lining, and trim. It sat over his ears like a felt bag, winter and summer.

And of course the family did nothing help soften the neighbours' resistance. His children came and went noisily and the grandchildren, with toys, carts, wagons, and tricycles spilling over the front lawn and sidewalk, cried, laughed, and yelled on their Sunday afternoon visits. The calm and peace of the Day of Our Lord were shattered.

Perhaps the Bennetts were so aloof because they were still in mourning their son Phillip, their only child, who had volunteered while a second-year Chemistry student at the University of Toronto and had been killed in 1917 at Vimy Ridge during the Great War. Now an aging couple, she ailing and he shuffling about, they existed alone in their house, with its overgrown front and back yards.

Whatever the reasons, the Bennetts and other neighbours continued to show their disgruntlement with the Stemeroffs by shunning them with dark looks, slammed doors, closed blinds—or silence.

But Stemeroff never seemed to internalize this treatment, though he knew what it meant. He had come to Canada in 1901 from Russia, from the regime of Czar Nicholas II, from bloody pogroms and violent attacks of the antisemitic Black Hundreds, from brutal army service in Siberia, and from the abject poverty of a Ukrainian village.

Moving from that past to this country had been no easy passage. Farming had failed and junk peddling had been a dubious livelihood. But Stemeroff had his own house now, secured by his hard-working half-dozen sons and daughters. The garden was thriving, his fruit trees were bountiful, and his chickens flourished.

Sitting in his back yard, he would say to himself in Yiddish: "So the neighbours are unhappy with a Jew in their midst and they don't talk to me? And *this* is antisemitism? Let me tell you about antisemitism, let me tell you what I lived through over there. *That* was antisemitism. My sergeant would order the Jewish conscripts to clean the latrines. He had a whip—and when he got drunk…. Until one day Isaac Borochovsky, a blacksmith and a shtarker (a strong, brave man), pulled it away and beat him senseless. Officers with their whores made us pull their carriages in races. We had to fight to keep our rations. Fistfights I could handle, but the knives…. And here Mr. Bennett won't talk to me? *This* they call antisemitism? The law doesn't say I can't live here. They don't like it? Too bad. They'll have to get used to it."

"Ah, there is going Bennett in his back yard."

"Hallow Meester Bennett," he shouted. "Nize day today, yezz? I soon bring for you fruits und wedge-tables."

But Bennett never acknowledged the gifts, and David Stemeroff continued to live in his house.

After some years, when Bennett was being moved to a retirement home, he looked at Stemeroff from the back seat of the car and raised his hand.

THAT OLD JEW

Election campaigns in Brantford during the 1930s included visitations by politicians and numerous rallies at the local Armories. Here, faithful Liberals, Conservatives, and CCFers, plus many curious onlookers, gathered at their separate conclaves in the hundreds to hear speeches from local party worthies and "distinguished visitors" dispensing nostrums they thought appropriate for local consumption. Surrounding them was the detritus of war: eighteen-pounder cannons, machine guns, rifles, swords, and awards, and on the walls, formal portraits of old militia commanders, compositions of senior officers, and medals garnered by soldiers of the Dufferin and Haldimand Rifles, the local militia regiment. Outside, on the promenade overlooking the Grand River, stood a small memorial to three local boys who had been killed in the South African War, some of Canada's sons who served the British Empire on kopje and veldt.

War and Remembrance were fitting symbols of the generation of veterans now assembled among others to hear the former Prime Minister, the Right Honourable William Lyon Mackenzie King, leader of the Liberal Party and of His Majesty's Loyal Opposition in the House of Commons, and, of course, contender for the premiership now at stake in this bitter election campaign of 1935. Richard Bedford Bennett and his Conservatives were on the defensive for failing to respond adequately to the Depression that for five years had taken the guts out of the Canadians and its generation of heroes whose jobs, farms, and hopes were drowning in a slough of despond.

Unemployment, anger, and anxiety stalked the nation, while in Brantford the giant Massey Harris, Cockshutt Plow, Waterous Engineering, Verity Works, and Coach and Body factories, and numerous machine shops were on short time, their capacity underused in a strangled economy. Proud machinists, tool and die makers, lathe operators, and foundry men stood each morning at the factory gates hoping to get the nod for a day's work. Back from overseas now sixteen years, the veterans among them were near middle-age, married with children and mortgages on homes whose values were plummeting. Down in Eagle Place and other working class districts of the city, they planted large vegetable gardens and fruit trees and raised chickens in backyard coops. They smoked 'make your own' fags and no longer even tried to hide their frayed collars and cuffs. They drank five-cent beer at the Legion and congregated on downtown street corners, as neighbours, army buddies, union comrades. But without regular work and pay envelopes, they had to scrounge for food, coal, clothes, and rent. And so they seethed.

Forty marching pipers playing "The Bluebells of Scotland" from the Ex-Imperials, veterans who had served far afield in Britain's armies, announced the arrival of the guest of honour. In his black suit Mackenzie King looked smaller than his five foot six height and was very pudgy. He smiled and waved to the crowd, some of whom cheered. Alongside him on his slow procession up the aisle came the mayor, Sam MacBride, and several aldermen, such as the highly popular John Patrick Ryan, as well as prominent local Liberal party men like W. Ross MacDonald. Leading clergymen and other "prominent citizens" were also part of the procession. They too waved and smiled as they advanced up to the platform.

David Stemeroff was there in the front row, having arrived at the Armouries even before the doors opened. A Liberal supporter since his early days in Berlin (now Kitchener) Ontario, he had distributed leaflets for King in 1908 and 1911 and had met—or been briefly introduced to—the Prime Minister, Sir Wilfred Laurier, who had shaken his hand while saying something like "my good man" and handing him a cigar. A cigar! And from this tall, elegantly dressed man who was the King of Canada! Well, not really, only Prime Minister. But to an uneducated immigrant from Czarist Russia, this constitutional distinction was at best vague. That cigar was never smoked: it was preserved for safekeeping in a little wooden box that David had crafted, only to be viewed in its crumbly state when he reminisced to his grandchildren about that memorable event.

Occasions like this one were sweet relief from the trade he plied. Or was it a business, this collection he made of old things, castoffs, going around his neighbourhood by horse and wagon and storing it in a barn. It had been different years ago, during the Great War, up in Mitchell where, with his partner Naftolin, he had been more successful and had shipped substantial tonnages of scrap by rail to the Hamilton brokers who sold to Stelco and Dofasco. That had all faded away in the Depression of the early 1920s and he was now much reduced. Family life, too, had deteriorated as his wife, Rifka, and children grew resentful of his business failure, one that limited prospects of good marriages and advanced education.

Stung by their disdain, David Stemeroff took refuge in his garden, a large plantation of vegetables and fruit trees, and in his egg-laying chickens, from which he reaped a weekly offering for his table. He worked out there daily, looking from time to time straight up into the sun, though he would sometimes rest on one of the handmade wooden benches he had scattered throughout his rows of vegetables. There he would smoke one of his handmade fags while peering off into the foliage, possibly remembering the old country and its poverty, violence, army service, family, and emigration. Maybe, too, he thought of his grandchildren, to whom he handed out pennies (he called them "coppers") from a bulging leather purse, saying "go you buy candy now." Then he would laugh and his eyes shone.

Now he was sitting in the front row at this political meeting in his blue serge suit and gray fedora. The platform party had entered and, pipers aweigh, they were coming slowly down the center aisle greeting, smiling, and waving all the way up to the stage where they took their places. Mackenzie King was front and centre. The noise was pretty loud until the assembled band struck up "God Save the King." The chairman, Mayor Sam MacBride, opened the proceedings. Somewhat of a Liberal himself, though with pronounced Labour leanings due in part to his job as a machinist at Massey's, MacBride took the opportunity to lambaste the current—and soon to be outgoing—Conservatives.

"What has Bennett done," he shouted, "for the workers of this country?"

"Our jobs have disappeared, many of us are on relief, and our kids walk around poorly. People can't even afford the twenty-five cents they need to see a doctor! So what have we got to hope for?"

After a few more minutes of similar thunderations, MacBride slammed the rostrum with a heavy fist and sat down, his face sweaty and red. He was replaced there by W. Ross MacDonald, once-defeated aspirant for the Brantford constituency in the House of Commons, who was to introduce King. A long-time Liberal, MacDonald had excellent connections in town. A smooth man, he knew who was who and who owned what. He knew the time of the day, and he deferred to the local ruling families. No maverick he, W. Ross, a war veteran himself, held forth with nostrums derived from the Laurier era, modulated by Mackenzie King's ideological barrenness.

Then it happened.

Instead of going directly over to the rostrum, King just stood up in front of his seat. He moved slowly to the edge of the platform, descended the steps, and walked over to Stemeroff. He smiled at him and held out his hand. This, in front of the entire assembly!

"Hello David. I'm glad to see you. How is your family?"

"Iz very gutt Meester Kink. I happy too. We gonna win dis time Meester Kink, you betcha."

By this time two thousand pairs of eyes were trained on the two figures, Mackenzie King and ... who? With raised eyebrows MacDonald turned to MacBride, who mimed a query to Alderman John Ryan. With furrowed brow Ryan turned to Reverend Stanley Johnston of First Presbyterian, who shook his head. Monsignor McDonough gently raised his hands, palms up. Union officials were bewildered. The platform party was stumped, flummoxed by the interruption of the proceedings.

"You think so, David? I'm glad to hear that."

"Yessir Meester Kink, I dink zo."

Just then the Mayor in desperation signaled the bandmaster to strike up, well, something to keep the crowd from growing restless. The bandmaster turned nervously to his musicians, tapped the stand, and whispered "Rule Britannia." Confused and angry at this summons, several bandsmen whispered back: "No. O Canada." The baton-wielder nodded and out came the anthem, somewhat discordantly, bringing the crowd to attention and song.

Stemeroff, already on his feet, looked up and smiled. He didn't know the words. So he stood there, shoulders back, head erect, eyes shining, feet together, and arms at his sides, next to William Lyon Mackenzie King, while up on the platform puzzled looks still went the rounds as the worthies whispered to each other:

"Who is he?"

"Do you know him?"

"Who is he?"

"Who *is* that?"

"Yeah," someone offered: "He's that old Jew who collects junk up on Terrace Hill."

Meanwhile, King, the "crusading opportunist," had seized the moment.

"Come with me, David, we'll go up to the platform," and took him by the arm.

So up they went, with the same two thousand pairs of eyes looking querulously on this odd procession of two. Stemeroff sat down amidst the honoured party right up front with King, MacDonald, the mayor, the Catholic prelate, and numerous Protestant ministers, union officials, aldermen, and other local worthies. He would have looked out over the crowd as proceedings advanced thinking … what?

What would have been passing through Stemeroff's mind as King, the hero of the moment, set about demolishing the Conservatives?

When the meeting ended, he walked out of the Armories right next to King, oblivious to the fact that the eyes of Brantford were still intently focused on him.

"Who *is* he?"

THE DAY BILLY
BUCAVETSKY DIED

They knew there was trouble in town the moment their father drove up and they saw him from the yard. He was white-faced and shook visibly. Without smiling or speaking he went straight into the kitchen, looked back, roared "stay out," and slammed the outside door. They heard him talking to his wife, who had been making supper.

It was 1943. The school yard was filled with talk about the Jerries, Krauts, Russians, the Marines, and stories about older brothers and cousins, uncles and fathers, overseas. The family next door, the Fullers, went limp one day and Jake was told not to go over there to cadge cookies off Mrs. Fuller. Her twenty-year-old son, Eugene, a deckhand on a Canadian merchantman, had been drowned with all his mates after his ship was torpedoed off Norway on the Murmansk run. For weeks "old man" Fuller wandered around his yard smoking his pipe, occasionally poking a shovel into the flowerbeds, and blinking a lot. Some months earlier, the Babineaus, who lived across the street, received a telegram saying that Freddy Galivan, the B's sister's husband—a corporal in the Royal Hamilton Light Infantry—had been killed at Dieppe. Larry B. told them later that his uncle's landing craft had taken a direct hit from a German gun.

"My uncle Freddy was blown to pieces."

In Jakes's small Jewish community of Brantford, none of the young men who had enlisted in the services had been killed yet.

There seemed to be lots of them in Air Force blue or Army khaki, because on the High Holy days the little shul was filled with uniforms. Joe Nisker and Sam Finkelstein had joined the Royal Canadian Air Force and stood praying with their fathers. Sam's uniform was better than Joe's because he was an officer, a bomber-navigator with a total war record (they found out later) of fifty missions over Germany. Jake Borlack was a Gunner's Mate in the Navy, served mostly on corvettes off St. John's, and made it up as far as Leading Seaman. Dave Moldaver joined the artillery, became a major and got a minor decoration after D-Day. Moe Noble got into some crack infantry unit, hit the beaches on D-Day, and was shot dead before he could get ashore. And there were others, like the three Rozansky brothers who volunteered for the Army; one of them got to be a Sergeant in the tank corps. The Rapaports, too, were in uniform, and so were Morris Romberg, Joe Lipovitch, and Al Lipofsky. The shul was filled with them and a few Jewish ser-vicemen who came from the nearby airbase on those festive occa-sions before they went overseas. The sons of peddlers, clothing storeowners, tailors, pressers, and scrap dealers joined up, trained, and "did their bit," as the saying went. Everybody was proud of them, especially the little boys, like Jake.

But for Billy Bucavetsky there was a special feeling. He did everything superbly well, it seemed. In school he was a first-class student, even in Latin, which nobody liked. When he finished Grade 13 he got most of the awards, including the coveted Webster prize for best all-round academic performance.

But it was in sports that Billy really stood out. He was a natural athlete. In hockey, he played centre for the city's Junior A team and would set the whole arena cheering as he deked his way down the ice, raced in from the blue line, passed to his mates, and scored with the kind of natural, effortless power and grace that would take him, probably, to the National Hockey League. This red-headed wonder dug the puck out of the corners and could mix it up with the toughest defencemen. As a football player, Billy was outstanding, and though only about 5' 11" and 180 pounds, he was built like a giant fireplug. An authoritative figure as defensive halfback for the Collegiate's seniors, and after graduation for the "Chieftains," a local Ontario Rugby Football Union team, Billy tackled with such power the collision could be heard all over the stadium. At basketball he was just as peppy and accurate. He 'had it' in all of these sports to which his fans paid attention. In others, like baseball, which they didn't, Billy also could turn in stellar performances. He played with power, zest, and genuine love for competition, winning, and roughhousing.

He had a temper, even though it didn't show too often. It would flare up at antisemitic remarks that were thrown his way at games: "dirty Jew," "sheeny," "kikey Ike," "Yid," and similar epithets. He'd had boxing lessons from the old coach at the Y known as "Boyo" Evans, and could deliver a right hook with devastating effectiveness. He had fists like sledgehammers. At a playoff football game in Kitchener he whacked a local boy around the mouth so hard the guy lost two teeth and got his nose broken. After some rough tackling he had called Billy a "filthy Jewboy." Billy—or "Red" as he was known to team mates—and his younger brother, Arnie, got a reputation around the school as bright students, generally affable guys, good athletes, but prickly personalities with heavy fists. They were respected, and most guys, recognizing that the Bucavetskys, when provoked, were capable of inflicting severe damage, chose not to tangle with them. Billy, therefore, was a figure of considerable stature in our community, especially among boys like Jake who were his junior by about ten years. Quite simply, he was their hero just as much as were Roy Rogers, Hank Greenberg, Superman, or The Shadow.

Could he fight, my God, could he fight! The stories were legion, especially the one about his singlehandedly beating up two local tough guys, the Anderson brothers, for their "Fucken Jew" remarks. Jake saw him in action only once, when he came to the rescue of Jake and his seven year old brother Ted, both playing in the park behind their house one summer morning when a neighbourhood lout, Bobby Green, then a husky eighteen year old, started smacking them around. "Ya dirty little Jews!" he hollered. "Get the hell outa' here. Go back ta where ya belong!" He caught Ted by the hair and whacked him with a backhand across the face, causing blood to pour from his nose. He let out a howl to rend the heavens and Jake, to wreak vengeance, came at Green, tiny fists flailing and shouting the most foul epithets he knew, receiving in return two powerful smacks for his efforts. He found himself lying on the ground with a terrific pain in his left ear and a rapidly swelling right eye.

The next thing Jake remembered was seeing carrot-topped Billy racing across the playground towards Green. Somebody must have gone to get him. Jake had seen many fights since then, and been in a few himself, but had never witnessed one of such ferocity. Billy punched with bone-breaking force, his fists bouncing Green's head back so often that it looked as if it was on a spring.

He broke Green's nose with a couple of right jabs and then went to work on his eyes, which soon became puffy and black. Green's face was badly bloodied within a few minutes and he continued to stagger while Billy pounded his face and upper body with maniacal ferocity. He was stopped just short of killing Green by the timely intervention of Serge Pellegrini and Ted Zahoryk, who had been watching the fight. They lived in the neighbourhood and they knew Billy well from having played on the same football team with him in high school and on the Chieftains.

At six feet two and about two hundred and fifty pounds, Serge was a veritable mountain of a man, while Ted was only slightly less hefty and very tough. After a few minutes they moved between Billy and the badly bloodied Green, who was on the ground spitting blood and groaning deeply.

"That's enough, Billy," said Serge firmly. "You gave him what he deserved and you've won. It's enough. Now call it quits."

"Bugger off," Billy screamed. "I'm going to kill this son of a bitch for what he did to these kids." He waved wildly at them and tried to push Serge aside.

"It's enough, Billy," Ted said calmly. "You've hurt the bastard, but it's enough." He put his hand on Billy's shoulder. "C'mon Billy. Let's take these kids home."

A wild skirmish followed. Billy punched at Serge, who dodged aside, while Ted threw a block at Billy's middle. All three toppled over and in seconds they were pinning Billy to the ground. They kept talking to him like friends, until finally he said "OK, OK. Let me up."

Billy took Jake and Ted home, one of them riding on a shoulder, a battered and bloody trio. The brothers had long since stopped their bawling, as they enjoyed the beating that Billy had given their tormentor. They had been saved and avenged by their hero, their *Yiddisher shtarker.*

Maccabees were they!

"OK, out you go," said Billy as he pulled them down from his truck when he got to their house. "And listen," he added, "learn how to fight, you little punkers. Learn how to fight!"

He got back into the truck and drove away. Not long after that he joined the Air Force and they never saw much of him, except for the few times he came home on furlough, the last occasion just before he went overseas.

His "old man," Yankel Bucavetsky, was less impressed with Billy's athletic performances than he was with his schooling, and kept urging his son to do better, study harder, forget about sports, and make plans for his future. Yankel was one of a dozen Jews in town who went round to factories and machine shops buying up scrap metal. He had started in this business shortly after he got to join Brantford's community of Ukrainian, Polish, and Russian Jews. He had an enormous respect for learning, and could discuss a page of Talmud, "a blot gemorah", with impressive skill, according to Boris Israel Tabachnik, who heard him do so in the occasional class they held in the shul's upstairs classroom.

Yankel hoped for something better for his sons than the junk business. While sorting out metals and dealing with the tough scrap brokers from Hamilton provided a living, it didn't provide status. He wanted his boys to go to university and become professionals: doctors, dentists, lawyers. Yankel worried a lot about them, their feistiness in particular, though (as we would have said then) he himself took crap from no one. A burly, square-built man with deep-set blue eyes, he had served as a conscript in the Czar's army at the front during the 1904-5 Russo-Japanese war and knew a thing or two about physical violence. While sorting out old farm machinery parts, car engine blocks, pipes and angle-iron in his yard down by the CNR tracks, past the roundhouse, he ruminated about their future.

After joining the Air Force in the summer of 1942, at age nineteen, Billy trained at Trenton, Wainright, and Shilo, and went overseas where he joined Bomber Command as a navigator. He was posted to a number four Bomber Group stationed at Harrowgate, trained on Lancasters, and was soon flying on raids over France and Germany. Yankel heard from him frequently but never knew details. His wife Basya was a quiet woman. She cried a lot after Billy left.

With many of their boys now overseas, the town worried. If the Tabachnik house was typical—and it probably was—people took to listening to the news by the hour. When it came on the radio, physical safety was at risk if the kids made any noise because Boris demanded absolute quiet. The Battle of Stalingrad and the even more decisive Battle of Kursk were followed with mounting passion, as it seemed that the Russians had turned the tide of war. The Red Army and its commanders became and remained among their greatest overseas heroes.

And there was bad news too, especially the murder of the Jews in Eastern Europe. Tabachnik's immediate family, who lived in Moldavia and Ukraine, had been shot, he found out later, along with thousands of others, by the Einsatzgruppe forces, with the assistance of local paramilitaries, in July 1941. But these events were remote, still largely unknown, and their lives in Canada were essentially undisturbed.

So when Boris walked into the house that day visibly suffering from some inner torment, the family knew that something unusual had happened. Never had Jake seen him so pale. He was in the kitchen with his wife for only a few minutes when Jake heard her scream, and then begin to sob. A shuffle of chairs followed, and another scream. Then she shouted, "Not Billy! When? *Oy, Gott zol Uphiten*" (May God take notice).

Billy's plane had been shot down a couple of weeks earlier during a raid over Hamburg and he, with the rest of his crew, were presumed dead. Their plane had been spotted crashing into the sea by Air Force observers. No parachutes. That morning a notice to this effect had been chalked onto the news blackboards attached to the side of the *Brantford Expositor* building on Dalhousie Street. There it was, under "Daily Casualties": "William J. Bucavetsky, R.C.A.F., missing in action, presumed dead." Boris had seen it on the way to the Post Office that morning, turned back, and had gone immediately to inform Joe Renkle, the shul president.

Renkle's furniture store was situated in the busiest section of the Colborne Street business strip and it had been there a long time. Louis Renkle, originally from a Bavarian village, saw himself as the leader in the community and was in the habit of lecturing the most recent immigrants in Canadian history, customs, and way of life, while admonishing them to get rid of their East European ghetto outlook and not behave like "greeners." That might be all right in Montreal or Toronto, he allowed, but not here in Brantford. A proud member of the local Oddfellows, he wanted no embarrassing questions at lodge meetings.

A hasty conference between Tabachnik and Renkle quickly revealed that, for some reason, Yankel and Basya had not yet been informed of their son's fate. The telegram that usually preceeded the public announcement of military casualties had not arrived, and the Bucavetskys were going about their normal affairs. Basya had been observed shopping at the market, they discovered after consulting others like Abe Kivenko, the town gossip, who also reported that Yankel was seen that morning driving out of his yard with a full load of scrap metal. Renkle, Tabachnik, and Kivenko quickly put things together: Bucavetsky was driving his truck to Hamilton to deliver scrap to the brokers, and would not be back until mid-afternoon at the earliest. It was ten a.m. and they would have to act fast to prevent anyone else finding out before Yankel got back and before Basya, Arnie, or anybody in the community walked past the *Expositor*'s blackboards.

They agreed on a plan and dispersed. Renkle marched promptly to the *Expositor*, barged into the offices, and demanded an immediate conference with editor Alex MacCready. The blackboard was quickly scrubbed clean of Billy's name. Meanwhile, Boris went directly to the rabbi's house to give him the news and to ask for advice. The rabbi promised to be available when needed and started to pray from the Book of Psalms, reading passages aloud in a tremulous voice. Leaving him to wrestle with the Almighty, Boris went over to Murafsky's grocery store, around the corner from the shul in the Jewish neighbourhood, to find out if anyone else had heard the news. With careful inquiries he learned that the secret wasn't out yet.

But the real question was how to go about breaking the news to the Bucavetskys. They could, of course, wait for the telegram announcing that Billy was missing to arrive at their house. But the fact that the message hadn't yet got there made them assume that it had gone astray. They decided, finally, to meet Yankel at his junk yard and tell him then and there. The task of informing him of Billy's probable death was delegated to Boris. They went to Bucavetsky's junkyard and waited.

Shortly after three o'clock, Yankel's truck lumbered into view and lurched to a stop. The three emissaries approached.

"Yankel," Boris said, "there has been an accident. It's Billy. He is missing in action."

Yankel's eyes widened and then blinked. He grabbed Tabachnik's coat lapels, pulled him to his chest and said slowly, "Tell me what happened."

"That's all I know, Yankel. Maybe Billy's plane was shot down. Maybe over Hamburg. Louis went to the *Expositor* office. They don't know either."

Yankel started blinking again and groaned. He moved back and forth as he did when praying in *shul*. "*Riboinoi shel oylem*," shouted Yankel, and, after appealing to The Master of the Universe, he strengthened his hold on Boris' coat. "His plane. Shot down. When?"

"We don't know, Yankel."

"Yankel, we are taking you home," said Renkle. "C'mon Yankel, let's go home. … Let's go home. Let's go now." Renkle put his hand on his shoulder.

"My wife, Basya, Basya! What shall I tell her?"

"C'mon Yankel," said Kivenko tugging on Yankel's jacket. "We'll all go with you. We'll all go and tell her."

But Yankel went home by himself. The three emissaries followed him and stood on the verandah of the house as the husband told the wife that their son was missing in action. Nobody went inside the house that day. They just waited on the verandah. As the news spread in town, they were joined by most of the community, including the rabbi.

Boris came home after that and sat in the living room. Jake saw him there when he got back from school a little after four o'clock. Boris had a handkerchief in his hand and his eyes were puffy.

"Hi, Pop."

Silence.

"Pop. Did something happen to Billy?"

"Aren't you supposed to go to cheder to-day?"

"Yes. I am going. But..."

"So, go. Get there, dammit. Learn something. You think life is a joke?" He was standing now.

"OK Pop, I am going." Jake went out the door, got on his bike and started down the lane out to the street. Then he saw his father standing on the verandah.

"Wait, wait, Jake. I'll drive you there." And he did.

The whole town mourned Billy. But not Jake. He didn't believe that Billy was dead, the fastest forward on the Junior A hockey team, the defensive halfback who hit so hard that bones shook, the shtarker who whacked the Andersons, and the Maccabee who saved him and his brother from a bad beating. No. No.

Do you think he believed that Billy could be killed by anybody? No way. Billy dead?

Naw! Billy was coming back. He knew it. He just knew it.

Years later, even after he realized that Billy had died that day, Jake would see a burly red-headed guy from a distance—and he wondered.

MASTER OF THE UNIVERSE

"Ribbonoi shel oylem," Isaac Ravnitzky intoned while looking out at his helter skelter junkyard. Through the filthy window he could see yard activity now at its nadir. His foreman, Mitro Zahoryk, was trying to get the heavily loaded four-ton Studebaker truck out across the CNR tracks for its journey to the Hamilton broker's yard. But the engine had stalled, leaving the truck athwart the tracks, and Zahoryk and his crew were pushing hard to get it off and out of danger. They were succeeding, but only slowly amidst shouts, imprecations, and a stream of colourful Ukranian, Yiddish, Russian, and Polish profanities.

But it was not this that was troubling Ravnitzky and leading him to appeal to the Lord himself. Master of the Universe indeed! It was the letter he had received that very day from his son, Fred, from his new home, a prison camp for captured Allied airmen in Germany. His Lancaster bomber had been shot down while returning to England from a raid over Hamburg, and Fred, a sergeant bomb aimer, had parachuted out with the rest of his crew.

He had landed near the Dutch border without injury, caught by local police, and held in a village lockup until he was picked up by a middle-aged Luftwaffe officer who, in perfect English, had declared gently: "You are now my prisoner. For you the war is over. Let me get you some lunch."

"My son, my son ... oh my son, Gott zoll uphiten." May G-d look down, he was praying, and protect his son, now two months into his captivity.

A knock on the streetside door interrupted his reflections and he lifted his head from the desk to see two large figures looming in front of him. He recognized them as local police detectives.

"Yes?"

"Where is your son? We're the police."

" So what? Why do you want him?"

"We want to talk to him."

"Why? What about?"

"Never mind! We want to talk to him."

"What for?"

"We want to *talk* to him!! Now where *is* he?"

"He's not here!"

"Bullshit! Where is he? We think he's evading military service—like a lot of you goddam Jews."

"Get the fuck out of here!" Ravnitzky, all five foot eight inches of him, was standing now, holding a length of lead pipe in his right hand.

"Get out, get out! Sonsofbitches, Mamzerim, Blady, Cholerias. *My son is in a German prisoner of war camp!!*"

The cops, startled, stepped back, wide-eyed.

"Yes, he's in a prisoner of war camp. That's where he is, you shits, you bastards, you sons of whores! Get out, get out, *get out!!*"

The two members of Brantford's finest left quickly, heads down, and shuffled towards their car, glancing quickly at each other and exchanging a few words.

"Go talk to him there," Ravnitzky shouted after them from the doorway waving his length of pipe. "Go to Germany, you filthy bastards, and talk to my son. … My son, my son … oh, my son … Ribboinoi shel oylem" (Master of the Universe).

Ravnitzky thought about Fred, barely twenty, small in stature, thin, with his huge eyes and twisted smile. Hoping to become a fighter pilot and get into the war early, Fred had joined the RCAF at age eighteen in May 1940 and had gone overseas a year later to join Bomber Command at a British air base. Shot down on his fifth mission, he was sitting now in captivity. What would the Germans do to him, a Jew? Would he ever come home? If so, when? And in what condition?

The Studebaker was now well off the tracks and Zahoryk was head deep under the engine hood looking for the trouble. Meanwhile, a freight train was moving several flatcars of new Bren gun carriers eastbound from the Ford plant at Windsor along the tracks towards Montreal. Yard activity resumed: workers sorted incoming scrap for iron, steel, copper, brass, tin, and aluminum, and threw them into separate piles.

Later that day, the phone rang and Ravnitzky lifted his head from his desk.

"Ravnitsky."

"Mr. Ravnitzky this is Police Chief Arthur Stanley. I want to apol—"

"Drop dead!" screamed Ravnitzky and slammed down the receiver. He marched out into the yard, picked up a hefty piece of angle iron and hurled it mightily against the storage shed, making a deep dent in the wall. He then grabbed a twenty pound sledge hammer and flailed away at a pile of tin scraps, sending them flying all around the junk yard.

"My son, my son," he sobbed. "Freddy, zindele, zindele mein." Now down on his knees, Ravnitzky shook and wailed. Zahoryk came over, picked him up and uttred words of comfort. Ravnitzky stumbled back to his office, picked up Fred's letter again, and read, as if to glean something new.

"Mr. Ravnitzky." A uniformed senior police officer, in a sharp uniform with rank shoulder badges gleaming and Great War service ribbons glowing, stood in the doorway.

"May I come in? I'm Chief of Police Arthur Stanley."

Silence.

"Please, may I come in?"

Silence.

"Mr. Ravnitzky, I've come to apologize for what happened this morning. We made a terrible—"

"My son. My son is in…."

"I know, I know. Mr. Ravnitzky, I know."

Ravnitzky slumped into his chair and covered his face with his huge, calloused, dirty hands and began to cry. Chief Stanley removed his cap and sat on the desk facing Ravnitzky, who was sobbing uncontrollably.

"Mr. Ravnitzky, three months ago our only child, Andrew, was killed on the beach at Dieppe. He was twenty, a lance corporal in the Royal Hamilton Light Infantry. He was our great joy, our only child. … So I think I have some idea what you're going through.

Ravnitzky looked up at the Chief.

The two men stared at each other in silence.

Ravnitzky slowly held out his hand.

"Ribboinoi shel oylem," he intoned. "Master of the Universe."

MORRICE

It was 1943. Most of the Brantford Jewish community's military-age men were already in uniform: several overseas in the Royal Canadian Air Force and Army, two in the Navy, a few in Zombie units, and the rest in various training formations. Married for only one year, Morrice Romberg had been conscripted into the Army in late 1942 at age twenty-four. He was a big handsome fellow, standing just over six feet and weighing nearly two hundred pounds. And strong! He worked with his father in their small junkyard where they stored the scrap metal, glass, paper, hides, and animal fat collected around town and in the nearby countryside in their old two-ton Dodge labelled "I. Romberg and Son, Scrap." Periodically, they sold what they had collected to Hamilton brokers, who sent over huge trucks to haul it away from them and the other Brantford junk dealers.

The I. stood for Isaac, a small, stocky man with over-bright eyes and a strangely constant smile. His wife, Leah, a very large woman, really ran the business, besides raising their four children, of whom Morrice was the youngest and dearest. When he married Jeanie Prokovnik, the talented and lovely daughter of a Hamilton broker in scrap—it was rumoured he had sold big tonnages to Japan in the 1930s—everyone was surprised that Morrice could make such a match because, though good-looking and pleasant, he was not very bright. Driving the truck and hurling heavy pieces of metal, bales of paper, and hides about was all he could do in the business. But he did this job well, stacking the heavy materials higher and higher in their crowded junkyard down by the CNR repair shops behind the station.

The young couple loved each other deeply, and when Morrice was drafted, they cried in each others' arms. Just before he left for Camp Borden to begin his basic training, she told him that they were to be parents in about seven months. He sank to his knees and grasped her gently around the middle. He brooded while aboard the troop train. When accidentally jostled by a fellow soldier, he snapped, threw the fellow, pack and all, full force against a seat and showed him his big fist. In the barracks he continued to brood, trained half-heartedly, read Jeanie's letters over and over again, talked to himself long into the night, and ate little.

At home, as Jeanie's time approached, complications developed and she spent much time in bed. Morrice got leave for the High Holy days and rushed back to be with her. In shul, on Rosh Hashana, he snapped again and suddenly grabbed Nachum Nyman by the throat, glaring into his eyes for several terrifying moments as the congregation gasped, then released his grip, smiling and laughing loudly.

"Varft im arois, der meshigener!" Throw the crazy man out! Nachman then yelled. "Varft im arois!"

Then, smiling and muttering, Morrice allowed himself to be hustled outside and went home alone. He threw stones at the lampposts along the way and waved at passing motorists.

Jeanie's condition was no better when Morrice's leave ended and he was obliged to return to Borden. She soon complained of painful symptoms to her mother-in-law, who took her to an old doctor, a total incompetent who misdiagnosed her condition.

A month later, Jeanie died in childbirth—the baby boy was stillborn—and her mother-in-law wrapped her in an old sheet awaiting the funeral. Morrice was summoned. But the poor girl's father, enraged at the in-laws' poor handling of her failing health and having taken his daughter's body to Hamilton for burial, refused to allow Morrice and his family to attend the funeral. Morrice mourned alone in the junkyard where he wandered all night, wailing and throwing things about. Police were called and neighbours tried to calm him down.

Compassionate leave ended and Morrice again entrained for Borden. Two days later, he assaulted his sergeant and had to be restrained by four members of the Military Police. They tossed him into a cell where he screamed constantly and hurled himself against the bars. In a straitjacket, he was finally brought to a psychiatric hospital in Hamilton, where he was to spend the rest of his life.

His father, Isaac, soon gave up his business and spent much time walking around town, his bright eyes glowing. He once fiercely grabbed Boris Israel Tabachnik by the coat and started to cry, yelling, "Boris, tell God to give me back my son!" then released his grip and ran down the street, leaving his grey fedora in the snow.

When Isaac died a few years later, he was buried in Brantford's Jewish cemetery. Leah would join him shortly.

After many years in the Hamilton asylum, Morrice died and was buried in a plot next to his parents. Jeanie, his beloved, lies alone only twenty miles away in the Hamilton Jewish cemetery.

ADVENTURES
WITH NUDNIK

When Jake entered the barn that chilly evening he was afraid, as usual, because it was a really creepy place: it was huge, dark, creaky, and smelly. It was an old structure, made of rough lumber—hand sawn back in pioneer days—and set way back on his grandfather's heavily treed property off on a hill at the edge of town. Birds flew in and out and bats hung from the rafters; the roof sagged in the middle, as if a giant had sat on top of it. The nearest house was a block away and there was usually nobody out on the road. Jake, a small twelve year old, was all alone and shivered in the dim light as he opened the door. He was going to feed his grandfather's horse, Nudnik, which was kept in his barn—in violation of municipal bylaws.

Jake's grandfather—he called him Zaida—was a junkman. He made a living collecting metal, bottles, paper, and rags, which he sold. He now lay sick at home with a bad case of the flu and could not go out to the barn to feed Nudnik, who had to have water, oats, and hay every day to keep her fit to pull the junk wagon. This ramshackle wooden vehicle, which tilted noticeably and dangerously to the left, was Zaida's conveyance, into which he loaded the old things that people left out at the curb for him every week as he made his rounds of the neighbourhood streets. Jake sometimes went out with him on these collections, listening to the stories Zaida told him about the old country, compulsory service in the Czar's army, and life in Canada when he arrived in 1901.

Jake loved his grandfather, a soft-spoken and kindly man whose wife was unhappy with him and showed her discontent by criticizing his every move, even screaming at him in the house. At meal times she often just dropped his plate in front of him silently, with a look of contempt. Jake felt sorry for Zaida and clung to him as a quiet old friend, one who was kind to his horse and to the chickens, geese, and ducks he kept in a big shed in the middle of his large garden. He tended his plants lovingly, staying out there for hours, planting and hoeing his vegetables, pruning and spraying his fruit trees, and tending to his flock. Jake liked to help him there, pulling weeds—sometimes by mistake some of the plants too—hoeing and picking fruit in the fall.

Jake needed a friend like Zaida because he often felt estranged and lonely. Jake's father usually came home only for meals and not until late at night, and his mother was overburdened with four children, work, and the organizations to which she belonged.

So helping his sick grandfather now was important to Jake, and while he was very frightened upon entering the barn, Jake was determined to feed Nudnik. He had seen Zaida do this many times and was pretty sure that he could, too. He would have to enter the stall with as little noise as possible, speak softly, fill the feedbag with oats, stroke the horse's mane, and, while cooing, put the feedbag over her neck. Then bring in the hay, four or five large pitchforks full, from the bale on the other side of the stall and fill the water trough.

But on this evening Jake's appearance somehow startled Nudnik. Maybe his nervousness caused her to shy and, as Jake tried to slip the rope for the feedbag over her neck, she suddenly reared back and then swung sideways, slamming him into the side of the stall. His head hit the boards hard. He saw stars, reeled backwards, and fell over unconscious with a deep gash on his forehead. Meanwhile, Nudnik rushed through the gate that Jake had left unlocked and out the barn door into the open, clattering down the lane at a fast clip. When Jake awoke about twenty minutes later, he was groggy and bloody, but anxious about Nudnik. He stumbled down to his grandparents' house.

"Nudnik's gone! Escaped! She got away from me when I tried to feed her."

"Oh, my God. What happened to you! Look at you! Oy, you've cut your head." His grandmother, whom he called Bubby in the Jewish tradition, looked aghast.

"Nudnik! Nudnik! Where is she?" Jake exclaimed. Thoughts of losing his Zaida's valued horse flashed through his mind.

"Oy, that horse, that horse," Bubby yelled. "I hate that horse —and the wagon and the junk. It's time the old fool gave it all up. Oy."

"But Bubby, where is she? Where is Nudnik?"

"Where? Who knows? But I saw her run through the neighbours's flower garden and on down the street."

Though still dazed and weak, Jake could think only of the horse. If she got away it would be his fault. He would have let his Zaida down and ruined his livelihood. Jake got to his feet slowly, hoping to run out of the house and look for Nudnik. But his head started spinning: he vomited and fell forward onto the kitchen floor. Before he lost consciousness he heard his grandmother yell out, "Call an ambulance!"

Jake was rushed to emergency and was admitted to a special unit for his concussion, which was judged to be serious.

Meanwhile, Nudnik was causing havoc and panic in the neighbourhood. She had galloped across several front lawns, ruining flowers, grass, and bushes, and had done particularly devastating damage to the roses on Mrs. Bennett's property—in addition to leaving a substantial deposit of manure. The Bennetts were furious and called the police.

In short order, a squad car arrived at Bubby and Zaida's house and the Sergeant informed them that keeping a horse in town was a violation of the law. Zaida would have to face charges in court and probably pay a hefty fine, as well as the costs of rounding up Nudnik and of damages to properties.

Over the next few days, Jake slowly improved in hospital, though he continued for some time to see double and to have recurring dizzy spells. "That's an awful blow you took, young fella," the doctor said. "We'll probably have to keep you here for another week or so."

Meanwhile, Zaida recovered from his flu and spent every day quietly at Jake's bedside, sometimes patting his hand and occasionally sobbing with worry about possible long term damage to his beloved grandson.

Nudnik had been recovered and was now lodged—legally—a few miles out of town, with a farmer Zaida knew.

Several weeks after these events, he was in court to face charges in front of Magistrate Richard Reville, known as "the Major."

"What do you have to say?" the Major growled at Zaida after the charges were read.

"Sir, your honour, I make my living collecting junk in my neighbourhood with my horse and wagon. I went to feed the horse and she got away. I regret this and will pay damages."

"Why do you keep your horse at home in violation of the law?"

"I don't walk so good, Sir, your honour. I got bad leg. Horse at home easier for me."

The Major glared down from the bench. "What's wrong with your leg?"

"Got shot, Sir, your honour, in time of Russian wars. Was long time ago. Soldier of the Czar Nikolai...."

The Major's face reddened slightly. He rustled his papers. "Where is the horse now?"

"In country, not at home, Sir, your honour."

"Be sure to keep it there, you hear, or you'll be back in court again! And what are you going to do about the damages?"

"I fix everything, Sir, your honour, myself. I fix everything."

"And I'll help him, Sir," exclaimed Jake, who had slipped into the courtroom.

The Major peered over his glasses down at Jake. "And who are *you*?"

"I'm his grandson, your honour."

"Why do you have those bandages?"

"I fell, Sir."

"Where?"

"In the barn, Sir."

"Where you kept the horse?"

"Yes, your honour."

"Ahmm, I see. You tried to help your grandfather?"

"Yes, your honour. You see, Sir, it was my fault that the horse got away. It's because I left the barn door open."

"Ahmmm." The Major again shuffled his papers, then adjusted his glasses, shifted in his seat, then looked out the window.

Silence.

"All right!" he exclaimed loudly to Zaida. "I find you guilty of this offence and fine you one dollar plus retrieval costs of one dollar. Or five days in jail. Repairs to damaged property to be completed within two months. Next case!" He banged his gavel and looked down at Jake with a quick, warm, smile.

After he paid the fine, Zaida and Jake walked out of the courtroom hand in hand. They got into a car and drove out to the farm to see Nudnik, who neighed and tossed her head when she saw Zaida.

"I'll keep her here and we'll visit every day. And you know what, Jake? I think it's time I bought a small truck to collect my junk. That way I can get around quicker and collect more of it. Also, it will leave more time for me to tell you stories about my life in the old country. Would you like that?" he asked.

Jake looked up and smiled. Even though his head still hurt a bit, he felt better.

PAPER TRAIL

Whenever Boris Israel Tabachnik travelled, especially any-where near the Canada-United States border (and with the possibility that he might want to cross over), or if he had any-thing to do with officials—Dominion, Provincial or municipal, all of them seemingly stern and uncompromising—he would carry what he called his "papers." He always knew exactly where they were, which was not the case for the location of anything else in his household. He kept them safe somewhere in the house—no one could figure out exactly where—so he could get to them quickly. They seemed to be his most important possession and he guarded them as if his life depended on their survival.

These "papers," however, were in reality a single green docu-ment: his Certificate of Naturalization. Boris treasured it not only because it was literally the only official document he possessed—his wife Anne, born in Berlin, Ontario, needed no such "papers," and, as befits a good Jewish wife, kept their marriage certificate—but also because it constituted proof that he was a Canadian, a legitimate member of this society, that he belonged here, had responsibilities to the country and was entitled to a share in what it had to offer. In short, it was proof that he was a *real* citizen.

Boris was so nervous about this document when traveling that he always kept it on his person, in the left back pocket of his trousers, a pocket with a flap that he always kept securely but-toned. And he never took it out except to show it to an official, or to put it back in its secret hiding place in the house. His family would only glimpse it during such official transactions, and Boris's son Jake had never actually held it in his hands—until recently, nearly forty years after it could no longer be of any use to Boris Tabachnik himself.

So when Jake took a good look at these "papers" for the first time, the certificate was in very sorry condition, having gone in and out of his dad's pocket countless times. It was badly faded and crumbly, despite the scotch tape that had been applied in several places to keep it whole. But it was still legible and it attested that in Brant County court, on Wednesday, October 16th, 1932, Boris Israel Tabachnik had become a naturalized Canadian. This had occurred only a couple of months following his eighth year anniversary in the country, and he had applied almost as soon as he had become eligible for citizenship.

Boris Tabachnik had no other document to establish who he was, where he came from, where he was born, and to whom. He had left his home country, which he always referred to as "Russia"—but which was Bessarabia, Moldavia, or Eastern Ukraine depending on the location of the borders—without "papers." He had no passport, no birth certificate, no police clearance, no work permit or identity card. And during his hurried flight from home, he had gathered none on his journey, which took him illegally and in considerable danger across the Dneister river into Romania. (Jake once lightly told him he was a "wetback," but Boris saw absolutely no humour in it.)

And because he had no "papers," Tabachnik was arrested repeatedly by the police, jailed, interrogated, beaten up—once pretty badly—threatened with torture, and humiliated. Once he was rescued by his brother, who had hired a well-known prostitute to "negotiate" with the local police chief for his brother's release. A fervent Zionist, he yearned to go to Palestine, where he thought he would be safe, where he could be a proud Jew and do the maximum good for his people. But because he had no "papers," the British authorities had refused to give him the necessary visa.

So when he presented himself to the officials who ran the Bucharest office of the Hebrew Immigrant Aid Society in the spring of 1924 to try to gain entry into Canada, Boris was a frightened and desperate man. He could neither return to "Russia," which he had left illegally, nor gain entry into Palestine. He was stateless. And, as arrests and their attendant brutality increased, time was running out for him. Canada—or, as he would have pronounced it, Kanade—was his hope of getting away from the Romanian cops who, it seems, suspected him and thousands of other Jewish refugees from the Russian Civil War and pogroms in Ukraine of being Communists, or other kinds of subversives. In any case, Romania was no hospitable a place for a Jew.

He had made it. The HIAS officials put him on their list and, after the physical examinations which he easily passed, he boarded the S.S. *Madonna*, an Italian passenger liner hired to take about 500 Jews to Canada, at Constanza, the Romanian port on the Black Sea. After about two weeks of passage through the Black Sea, the Aegean, the Mediterranean, and the Atlantic, he landed at Halifax on August 24th, 1924, where, asked by officials whether he'd prefer to go to Montreal, Toronto or Winnipeg, he chose Toronto, probably because one of his shipmates had recommended it. Not that it really mattered to him: Boris didn't know a soul in all of Canada.

Still no "papers," though, save a receipt that proved he had been a ship passenger, and maybe a chit attesting that he had passed the final Government of Canada physical exam in Halifax. But he had nothing that, in his eyes, fully legitimized him as a person. He took evening English classes at Egerton Ryerson school across the Grand in West Brantford. He could get married, as he did in August 1927; he could father a child, as he did four times; he could join a shul, the B'Nai B'rith, the Canadian Jewish Congress, the Zionist Organization of Canada, and the Independent Order of Odd Fellows (his family could never understand this affiliation). He could open a business, buy a car, pay taxes, and rent a house. But none of these, he believed, gave him complete legitimacy in the eyes of the law, and he would quail at the sight of a policeman. Jake once observed that when a soldier wanted to bum a cigarette, Boris held out the entire package with hands quivering.

In a world where there was a right order of things, real people had "papers." His children had them in the form of Ontario birth certificates, school and university graduation diplomas, letters of commendation, commissions in the Royal Canadian Navy (Reserve), and other such "official" documents which he kept locked away somewhere.

And so, as his children grew up, they would hear from time to time that, for a special reason, their dad was going to get out his "papers," the slowly disintegrating but always precious naturalization certificate which he believed gave him legitimacy and security. With his "papers," Boris was a somebody; without them he still saw himself as that skinny, unarmed youth running away from drunken Cossacks or sword-swinging gangs of hooligans and murderous antisemites, swimming across a muddy river, hiding from the Romanian police, longing to go to Palestine, but ending up alone on a Halifax dockside.

Boris Israel Tabachnik might never have felt entirely secure with his "papers" on his person, but before going on a trip he always made absolutely sure that his Certificate of Naturalization was safely buttoned into his left rear pants pocket.

BAGPIPE BAR MITZVAH

Boris Israel Tabachnik stubbed out his cigarette—he favoured Sweet Caporals—as Rabbi Gelder walked into his store, Tabby's Men's Wear, an upscale haberdashery on Brantford's Colborne Street.

"Shalom Aleichem, Rabbi. Your family is well, I hope." Boris was smiling.

"Baruch Hashem. Thanks be to God," the rabbi replied.

But he was not smiling. "Mr. Tabachnik: is it true?"

Boris winced. The news had gotten all over town.

"To what might you be referring, Rabbi?" Best to go slow on this one.

"Mr. T., I've heard that you plan your son's bar mitzvah celebration for a downtown hall—instead of … in our synagogue."

"Well, Rabbi, you see—"

"Mr. Tabachnik. Please reconsider! The food will not be strictly kosher."

"Well, my wife and I have made arrangements with Bolaslavsky, the Hamilton Jewish caterer, to bring in—"

"This would be a scandal, Mr. Tabachnik, a scandal. I must strongly disapprove."

"Now, Rabbi. My views on this matter are well known. We do not keep a strictly kosher home and I think it would be hypocritical of us to—"

"This is an outrage, Mr. T., you cannot—"

"Well, rabbi, I have no wish to offend …."

But Rabbi Gelder suddenly turned away and walked out.

Boris lit a Sweet Cap, but what he really needed was a stiff drink.

Damned if he'd let the rabbi stop him. The shul was too small for the big do he had in mind. So he had made inquiries and found his answer to the kosher food question.

A venue was another matter. The hall above the Ex-Imperial Veterans' large building on Market Street was the only place in town the Tabachniks could find to rent for the bar mitzvah celebration. The Independent Order of Foresters, the Oddfellows, the Masonic Temple, the Knights of Columbus, the Moose, the Elks, and all other lodges whose premises he tried to rent had turned him away. And the synagogue's hall was just not adequate for the throngs of people the Tabachniks intended to invite for the celebration.

The new shul was only in the planning stages, heart attack-inducing rows having taken place between various members who deemed themselves experts in the design of the structure. Factions were forming: the Thursday night poker group had split three ways; lifelong friends were not speaking to each other; rabbis near and far were consulted and the Canadian Jewish Congress sent up a mediator from Toronto—all to no avail. The highly esteemed Rabbi Levine was brought in from Hamilton to plead with the contesting parties and appeal for peace in the name of the Patriarchs. But "Sit geholfn vii a toiten bankess": It helped like a dead healing cup.

So, on the designated Saturday night following Jake's nervous and clumsy performance in the shul reading the Torah, singing the haftorah, and giving a lengthy verbal dissertation (written by his mother) on the portion of the week, the festivities were begun, with the veterans of the Boer War and of the First and Second World Wars, as well as of numerous colonial actions between, in silent attendance.

Among them were veterans of the Coldstreams and other Guards regiments, the Indian Army, and the Territorials. The largest contingent, however, were Scots, whether Highlander or otherwise, who in their Canadian setting foregathered at the Ex-Imperial Hall to celebrate their Scottishness. Here they formed a band of some forty bagpipers and about fifteen drummers dressed in the colourful uniform of the Gordon Highlanders. Together with the bands of the local Canadian Legion and the Brant, Haldimand, and Dufferin Rifles (the local Militia regiment), as well as some from neighbouring places such as Hamilton, whose Argyll and Sutherlands regularly came over to Brantford. Even the Toronto Scottish and the 48th Highlanders would sometimes appear for the "Home" tattoo put on every few years at the Fair Grounds. Then, indeed, would North British Hearts soar as the massed bands gave forth with "The Bluebells of Scotland," "Will Ye No Come Back Again," "Major Manson's Farewell to Clashantrushal" and other celebrated marching tunes. These now-aging men, their families, and the curious, including neighbourhood kids, would be stirred by such sounds, as well by the colours of the tartans, tunics, tams, dirks, sporrans, and gaiters of the men—most of them sporting rows of medals—proudly parading before the appreciative crowds.

Marches and countermarches and the forming of squares amidst such cadences or strathspreys as "John MacFadyen of Melfort" and "Dorator Bridge," reels like "Alex C. MacGregor" and "The Rejected Suitor," slow airs like "Loch Ramoch" and "Colin's Castle," and the rousing pibroch "The Munro's Salute," brought tears to the eyes of the men who had faced death for Queen and country in Afghanistan on the South African veldt and kopje, in the trenches and at the Somme, Passchendaele in Flanders, and during "the Hundred Days."

All hearts went out to them on these occasions, especially when they paraded, heads up, shoulders back, arms swinging, Union Jack unfurled, old regimental flags held high; then "eyyyyes right" past the reviewing stand on November 11th to the Cenotaph. Here they stood as prayers were intoned, speeches droned, and the last post and reveille sounded. Then to attention, right turn, forward march and left wheel back towards the Legion and the Ex-Imperials for a "wee dram," "slangeavor," reminiscences, and songs—and another shot of whisky or two, to drive out the cold—"just that, mind"—and the memories of Scotland the brave. Aye! And the songs long into the night: "Just a wee doch'n doris. Just a wee one, that's aa ... Just a wee doch'n doris before we gang a war." "Ay belong to Glasgow, dear ol' Glasgow toon. What's the matter with Glasgow, all the warld is spinnin' roond" … and many more.

And another wee dram, "just to keep out the cold, mind."

Several pipers dressed in full regalia were practicing as the first guests to the bar mitzvah mounted the stairs to the hall Boris Tabachnik had rented on the second floor. From below, the wailing, squeaking, and wheezing of bagpipes being filled with air and tuning up wafted upwards from open windows. A piper would play a few bars of, say, "I am a Young Man that Lived with My Mother" amidst guffaws and shouts from his mates.

Meanwhile, at the bar mitzvah upstairs, festivities began with the usual moytsi, the blessing over bread, which was offered by Uncle Berel from London. While the meal progressed, the music below became more synchronized as more pipers arrived and tuned their instruments. Guests began looking at Boris in mild amusement and were wondering at the juxtaposition of bagpipes and blessings, of Scots and Jews, of tartan kilts and blue suits, of old battles and old fears.

Of the call of the heather and the yoke of the Torah.

By the time the inevitable speeches began, the ensemble below had reached its full size: all 40 pipers and 15 drummers had arrived. When Boris stood up to address the sea of faces before him, the band had assembled in full array in the side street right next to the building, and loudly struck up the sprightly march "Wi a Hundred Pipers." By this time, Boris was only part-way through an emotional Zionist spiel, followed by a quick run through—in English, Yiddish, and Hebrew—of Jewish history, beginning with the Roman conquest of Palestine, the Middle Ages, the Modern period, and Theodore Herzl's revelations, and ending up with David Ben Gurion. And as he spoke, the pipers below delivered up "Scotland the Brave" and "Blue Bonnets over the Border," pausing only for refreshments of the amber liquid amidst loud shouts and preparations for the dancing that was soon to begin.

And it did, with the best pipers (including Andy MacLaren, Great War vet of the Royal Scots Fusiliers, whom Jake knew from his neighbourhood) calling forth to do the honours. And then came three young girls in full kilt to dance between swords brought into the hall and laid down on the floor. The "Flora Macdonald" was performed, though the level of artistic perfection rapidly declined as the dancing proceeded, as tipsy pipers from below learned of the availability of free whisky upstairs. Several of them joined the celebrants, thus discouraging the girls from continuing.

Not to be overwhelmed by this friendly invasion, a dozen Jewish youth formed a circle around the Scots and started dancing the hora to the loud tunes of the hired bar mitzvah band. Pipers giving out "The Road to the Isles," were now competing with "Hava Nagila," "Mayim, Mayim," "Tzena Tzena," and other spirited tunes, the one extolling Scottish maleness and history, the others celebrating the modern Hebrew revival. Amidst loud cheers and rhythmic clapping of hands, Maxie Wexler added to the mix by fairly decent renditions of Ukrainian and Russian kazatskas. Almost a conjuncture of themes, a merging of ideals, a sympathy of values.

Meanwhile, the bar mitzvah celebration continued as more food appeared, alcohol was consumed, speeches passionately delivered (mostly in Yiddish and often punctuated by loud applause from the tipsy Scots bandsmen who appeared upstairs in increasing numbers).

Boris Tabachnik and his family rejoiced, Rabbi Gelder remained steely, the Ex-Imperials celebrated, and the guests were well fed.

LAURIER'S CIGAR

"God damn communists! Cholerias, Paskudniks, Zollen zai brennen!!

While thus upbraiding the radical left as cholera-bearers, thoroughly rotten persons, and worthy of burning in Hell, David Stemeroff stormed into the kitchen with these Russian and Yiddish epithets that would have been far worse if Jake's grandmother had not been present.

Tie askew, shirt besweated, jacket unbuttoned, and fedora atilt, David slammed the door, clumped over to his chair by the table, and sat down.

"Zollen zai brennen! God damn communists!" he shouted at the glass of water she was putting in front of him.

"Shah! Voss iz der mere mitt iyr?" She banged on the table.

"I'll tell you what's the matter with me—and don't order me to be quiet in my own house. The farkakte, shitty communists..."

"Shah! What's with the communists?"

"Curvehs, all of them whores and bastards, the mamzerim!"

"Stop already with the swearing. You're not in the barn now. Drink some water. What happened?"

"I went to the meeting you told me to attend."

"And so?"

"It was a farkakte *communist* meeting! Mamzerim with their son of a bitch Stalin. May he...." David was standing now, ready to pour out still more wrath upon Moscow when Louie, their son, entered.

"What's going on?"

Gerald Tulchinsky

"I'll tell you *comrade* Leibele, friend of the Kremlin, Lenin, Trotsky, Stalin. Workers' Paradise—shit!"

"David! *Please!*" She turned to Jake. "He went by accident to their meeting. The man on telephone say going to be meeting tonight. He say Liberal party meeting at union hall."

"What Liberal? It was not the Liberal party. It was a labour meeting at the union hall, Labour Progressive party meeting! I went to the wrong meeting too. You told me the man on the telephone said the labour meeting was at the Legion, but it was the shmucky Liberals."

Silence.

"So shoot me. I mixed up a little. I have to keep track of these meetings? I don't have enough to do? I have to keep track? Politics feh! Labour is Liberal, Liberal is Labour, no?

"Not same thing! Ribboinoi shel oylem, may the Master of the Universe look down. God damn communists take away everything and—"

"Ma, Liberal is not labour and labour is not Liberal. Mackenzie King is not Joe Stalin and Karl Marx is not Wilfrid Laurier."

"Laurier! You got something to say about Sir Wilfrid Laurier?" David remembered the friendly Prime Minister—the Prime Minister of Canada no less!—who gave him a cigar at an election rally in Berlin, Ontario, in 1908.

"Laurier was an idiot, a tool of the capitalists. He sold out the working class."

"He was my friend. He shook my hand, asked my name and gave me a cigar." David moved to the cupboard and took out a small box. "He gave me a cigar, this cigar!"

"Yeah, you told me before. A cigar makes a friend? Pa, this cigar is a symbol of his power over you, of the bosses' exploitation, of subjugation, of imperialism, and—"

"No! This cigar is for me a promise, a passport, a ticket."

"A ticket? A ticket to what? Did it get you a job? a business? a house? a future? No! You have try to make a living with horse and wagon collecting bottles, picking up rags, hides, paper, and old iron, and wait for those thieves, those brokers from Hamilton, to give you a few dollars for it…. In Russia there is a better future."

"In Russia is a better future? Let me tell you about Russia, the Army, Siberia—"

"That was the old Russia. Russia is a new world now. The future is there!"

"*Here* is the new world. Here! This cigar is the new world. *This* is the future."

"Pa, I got laid off today. Massey Harris is closing down the tractor production line. A hundred and fifty of us are out of work now."

Silence.

Silence.

"I made a nice cabbage borscht today. Come eat."

Silence.

David turned away. He went to the cupboard and put the cigar back in its place, then out the back door to his garden. He took out his tobacco pouch and cigarette papers, rolled himself a fag, took out his matches, struck one on his shoe, and lit up. He walked over to one of his benches and sat down. He took a few drags and looked over at his fruit trees, his vegetable patches, his chicken coop, and thought about his barn, where he kept his wagon, stabled his horse, and stored his bottles, rags, hides, paper, and old iron.

Next week, the brokers were coming from Hamilton to buy. They would drive a tough bargain.

KIVENKO'S PLAQUE

There are places across Canada where small Jewish communities once thrived, strung out like fringes of a huge tallis, in small cities and towns where Jews made their livings as peddlers, storekeepers, and junk collectors. From all over Eastern Europe they came and settled throughout the vast country during the great immigration waves of the early twentieth century. Brantford in southwestern Ontario was once such place in the 1940s, an industrial city of some 30,000 people, among them some 200 Jews in fifty families.

From villages and small towns in the backwaters of Russia, Lithuania, Austria, and Poland they came together in uneasy, though necessary, communion to pray in the new but modest synagogue, Beth Baruch, named in memory of Baruch (Billy) Bucavetsky, killed in July 1943 while on active service with the Royal Canadian Air Force. The shul was built in 1947 on Waterloo Street in close proximity to the Jewish neighbourhood, and just around the corner from the old shul, a ramshackle structure that was converted into a Hungarian Baptist church.

One Sunday night—not a dark and stormy one—just an ordinary night, not too dark, not too bright, not too stormy, not too pleasant, just a regular Sunday night in this Jewish community, a terrible thing happened. A plaque honouring Abe Kivenko, immediate past president of the shul, was removed from the synagogue's wall. Nobody knew who was the first to find out; maybe there was a minyan the next morning; maybe the shamess came in on his caretaker duties to pick up the Sabbath prayer books and the talesim strewn over the benches; maybe the rabbi arrived on some mission; maybe a stranger came by and decided to rest for a few minutes. Who knows?

Maybe even one of the legendary lamed-vavniks, the thirty-six righteous persons who, according to Jewish tradition, pass through this world, and by their deeds uphold its continuing existence before the Almighty, stopped here and witnessed the loss. It could even have been Elijah the Prophet himself, passing through on a pre-Passover tour, possibly to scout out the Jewish houses he would visit on that holiday. It didn't matter. Somebody found out early Monday morning, and by ten o'clock the news was all over town.

There was no shortage of broadcast media at their community's disposal, not including radio (television was not yet available). Numerous persons were prepared, on receiving such serious news, to rush to their telephones and spend hours relaying information, impressions, gossip, reflections, interpretations, slander, and outright lies to eager listeners. One person was so well known for such broadcasting that she was called "CKPC," after the local radio station. There was old man Murafsky and his wife Rivkah, at whose grocery store not far from the shul such stories collected and stored themselves like the cans of preserved food and stacks of Stanfield underwear on its rickety shelves, or the pickles in the enormous barrels in the basement, to be picked up by his Jewish customers as they entered, sidled up to the counter and asked "What's new in town"? "Nu, vos hertzach?" "Vos machstu?" Murafsky would raise his hands, smile, wince, mumble, roll his eyes, puff out this cheeks, shrug his shoulders, and laugh loudly, thereby hinting that indeed something was up. Somehow the news would come off the shelves, up from the pickle barrels, and into his customers' shopping bags to be taken home and spread around the neighbourhood streets and kitchens.

The best broadcaster in town was Abraham Kivenko, one of the Colborne Street ladieswear storeowners. Everyone knew that Abe Kivenko regularly disseminated information, misinformation, rumours, fabrications, speculation, and calumny from his perch in

Greco's Grill, a downtown greasy spoon, where he met some of the other Jewish storekeepers, like Boris Tabachnik, on a daily basis. Abe told stories about everybody—and what he didn't know for sure he invented.

Was the rabbi's wife not seen in shul last Sabbath? Kivenko's answer: she's pregnant again. Did an engagement break up between two local soon-to-be-weds? With lowered voice Abe related that in the locker room at the Hamilton steam bath, where some of the Jewish guys gathered after poker, he'd noticed that the intended groom's penis was unusually small and that the bride's father was informed by—who knew? Did somebody's son get a police summons for getting caught late one night with a bottle and a broad parked down beside the swamp road, otherwise known as Humpers Hollow? Abe told the story—with embellishments galore—to ready listeners. Did Billy Bucavetsky, our local Jewish star athlete, bash in the faces of the Anderson brothers for some "dirty Jew" remarks? Abe would describe the incident as a bar room brawl in which Billy was roaring drunk.

There were no limits to this man's lying, his distortions, his purely vicious nature. His malevolence, innuendo, and dark hints poisoned the town so badly it was a wonder, Boris Tabachnik often reflected, given the capabilities of some of the local Jews, that Abe wasn't roughed up verbally, or even physically.

So when his plaque on the shul's wall of honour was torn off and removed that Sunday night, there was quiet contentment throughout the community that the son-of-a-bitch had received his due. In fact, everybody had resented having it there in the first place.

So when his term as shul president ended after only a few months, amidst almost constant community acrimony and unrest, Kivenko rushed approval for a plaque through a tempestuous board meeting, disguising it as "improvements." He had one made at his own expense and hired workmen to hurriedly affix it on the shul's Wall of Honour. It read:

ABRAHAM J. KIVENKO, ESQ.
PRESIDENT BETH BARUCH

SYNAGOGUE
Sept. 1950 to Dec. 1950
HONOURED BY ALL

Abe had many enemies. Several of them, including Ben Kranzler and "Mack" Brauer, had done the deed. How do we know? Boris Tabachnik had found out. How did he find out? He sniffed around. He knew the town. He knew its characters as well as anyone and he put things together.

Downtown, he walked slowly up Colborne Street, where he recognized all the storekeepers, and around Market Street and up Dalhousie, past the Post Office, stopping to chat wherever he saw a friendly face. He spent even more time than usual in Greco's Grill schmoozing with the drifters and schnorrers coming through town, the haberdashers, shoe salesmen, and ladieswear storeowners. At shul meetings he watched who was talking to whom. At a B'nai B'rith stag in the shul's basement for Jack Moldaver, who had rejoined the Canadian Army as an artillery Captain to fight in Korea, he overheard some of the younger guys talking, laughing, and whispering. He conferred with his cronies. He ruminated and within a week he had it nailed down. But he kept his mouth shut.

What to do? The insult to Kivenko was serious, of course, but in Boris' eyes the main things was to avoid deeper communal animosity than had already occurred. There was awful unrest in town. If Kivenko's plaque could be removed, whose plaque was safe? The Wall of Honour could become decimated, leaving nothing but a series of empty spaces where, now, dozens of brass plates inscribing the deeds of former shul presidents and generous donors of prayer books and monies for the building fund glittered. Boris wanted to close the case and get the community up for the really important things, such as the next United Jewish Appeal campaign and the hiring of a new rabbi to replace Rabbi Fisher who, to everyone's relief, had been "called" to the pulpit in nearby Guelph.

So Boris approached Louis Renkle and Max Weiss, and, in deep communion in the rear of Renkle's furniture store, the three devised a three-part strategy. Boris' job was to placate Kivenko, who was loudly threatening dire consequences all over town unless the plaque was found and replaced. He had asked his lawyers, the firm of MacLachlan, Ryerson, Waterous, MacCready and O'Toole, to begin legal proceedings against the synagogue—itself a scandal, as it would involve non-Jews in an internal Jewish dispute. Renkle, meanwhile, would attempt to deal with the culprits, to retrieve the plaque and have it reattached. Weiss, the richest and most influential Jew in town, would enlist their feckless rabbi to try to spread peace throughout the community, which was talking about nothing else but Kivenko's missing plaque and the implied threat to the Wall of Honour.

But the campaign plan ran into trouble from the very start. Kivenko was adamant, and so all of Boris' efforts failed to dissuade him from suing. The rabbi's attempts to calm the community were only marginally successful, as acrimony bit deeply into its soul. And Renkle's negotiations with the plaque thieves, Kranzler and Brauer, met with loud denials and dark smirks. Worse still was the news from the shul's secretary that the minute books had been tampered with and the page on which he had recorded the hasty decision to allow Kivenko's plaque was missing: it had been torn right out of the book.

"Ribboinoi shel Oylem!" (Master of the Universe!) Boris was so distressed he could hardly eat his normally hearty suppers. What to do, what to do? With Renkle he drove to nearby Hamilton to consult with the distinguished and widely revered Rabbi Levine, a pious and learned man of about eighty, who had headed that city's oldest Orthodox synagogue for over forty years. They pleaded with him to make a visitation to Brantford, and with the authority and prestige he enjoyed as the "chief rabbi" of the region (embracing communities in the areas bordering western Lake Ontario, eastern Lake Erie, and the *entire* Grand River valley), he could induce the community and the defiant warring parties to follow the path of peace. With a quiet sigh, the good rabbi agreed to come.

His visitation began with prayers and ended with pleas for harmony in this deeply riven community. Learned references to Abraham, Isaac, and Jacob; to Sarah, Rebecca, Rachel, and Leah;

to Moses and the Judges; to all the Prophets; to Kings Saul, David, and Solomon; and to the sages and all the learned rabbis of the Mishnah, Talmud, and Midrash were to no avail.

"Sit geholfn vii a toiten bankes" (this helped like a dead healing cup), said Boris in completed disgust as he viewed the congregation's stony faces after the exhausted Rabbi Levine departed, slumped in the rear seat of Renkle's big Buick. With two fundraising campaigns looming, the failure of the peace mission was a sign that they would have a tough time getting people's minds off the scandal of public hearings soon to take place in Magistrate's Court over the theft of Kivenko's plaque. Already news had leaked out as far afield as Toronto, and Boris had been phoned by worried officials at the Canadian Jewish Congress who were concerned about the public relations aspects of the case. What if the affair were reported to the press? What would Ontario's Jew-haters make of the whole business?

In due course, therefore, notwithstanding all of these attempts at concession, conciliation, and negotiation, the case came to court before old Magistrate Richard S. "Dick" Reville, whom everyone called "the Major"—he had won the Military Cross for bravery in the Great War)—and who knew every character in town, including all the local drunks, brawlers, wife-beaters, whores, bootleggers, rapists, thieves, and other offenders against the King's peace. He knew all about "the reasonable man," the rules of evidence, "probable cause," and other tricks of the lawyer's trade. He knew the difference between fact and fiction, credible witnesses, and so forth. After about an hour of loud and confusing testimony from various witnesses in his busy court, he leaned over the bench and sharply asked Kivenko what value he put on the plaque. Caught off guard, Abe replied: "One hundred dollars," which had been the cost to him.

"Fine," said Reville. "I order the synagogue to pay Mr. Kivenko one hundred dollars for the loss of his plaque. I order that the synagogue permit him to erect a new plaque in place of the one that was removed. And, finally, I further order that all costs of this action be paid by Mr. Kivenko. Next case."

Kivenko, went out of court $100 richer, but, when all the bills came in, poorer by about $1,000 in court costs and legal fees. However, he had the right to put up another plaque—and this he did very soon. It remains on the shul's wall to this day. It reads:

ABRAHAM J. KIVENKO ESQ.
PRESIDENT BETH BARUCH
SYNAGOGUE
Sept. 1950 to Dec. 1950
A PLAQUE FOR ALL MY ENEMIES

IN BOLOTENKO'S GARDEN

Bolotenko was usually hunched over among his plants, weeding the beds or picking his harvest in September, as Jake and his brother, Ted, walked down the hill in the late afternoon to attend cheder, their Jewish religious school. It was held at the shul, upstairs in one of the large rooms of the old ramshackle building, and run by "Rabbi" Charloff.

Charloff brooked no nonsense or incompetence in reading the Hebrew prayers on which he concentrated his efforts. He would whack an offending boy across the hand or face with a long heavy ruler (Jake thought it had a steel edge) whenever the victim was too slow in reading, or had badly garbled one of the familiar passages in the prayer book.

Bolotenko's garden was on Jake's accustomed route from Graham Bell Public School. Their neighbourhood on Terrace Hill was pretty solidly WASP, where people with names like Gale, Hicks, Cooper, Webster, and Mitchell attended the United, Anglican or Baptist churches, professed animosity toward Catholics, and called people with other origins "foreigners," "hunkies," or "Jewboys," epithets often preceded by profane adjectives.

Down the hill, however, and in another school district, there lived a mixed ethnic population comprised mostly of Hungarians, Italians, Poles, and Ukrainians who worked in the nearby factories. They congregated, when at leisure, in their recreation and cultural centres, called "halls." Most of them had pronounced political affiliations, which bitterly opposed each other, and minded their own affairs, and attended Saint Joseph Catholic Church or the Orthodox Church.

Many of the residents of this district had wonderful vegetable gardens in their yards, which in late August and September gave up a cornucopia of tomatoes, peppers, cucumbers, string beans, cabbages, carrots, zucchini, beets, and other delights. Fruit trees yielded huge quantities of pears, plums, cherries, and apples; chicken coops produced a daily supply of eggs.

Bolotenko's garden was more public than most others in this neighbourhood because it was situated on a triangle of land at the conjuncture of four streets below the elevated tracks of the main line of the Canadian National Railway. But its basic quality stood out starkly against the industrial grime and the meanness of the streets in this area. And as the Tabachnik brothers moved down the hill towards their daily rendezvous with Yiddishkeit, they were struck by the verdancy, productivity, and the labour invested by Mr. B. and his wife. The brothers sometimes lingered by the wire fence surrounding this place because, often, the Bolotenkos would offer them an apple, pear or plum, and smile when the boys said "thanks."

Bolotenko's garden was not only an oasis of greenery, but also became a refuge for these brothers as they tried to negotiate their way through the rough neighbourhood to cheder. Usually, they took wide detours in order to avoid encountering the gangs of hostile boys who knew who they were and where they were going. The hostiles often waited for them, ready to fight. Because of the imbalance of forces—the attackers usually outnumbered the attacked two or three to one—these encounters were often dangerous. In addition to fists and sticks, sometimes even slingshots were used, with gruesome results.

Jake got hit once by a stone just above his left eye and fell down stunned and bleeding badly. He lost consciousness. Thinking Jake a goner, his brother picked up a heavy stick and lay about him with brutal effect to drive off the four attackers, yelling: "You bastards killed my brother!"

He pulled Jake out of the railway underpass back towards Bolotenko's house. Jake staggered along with him, groggy and temporarily blinded by the blood flooding into his eyes. They got to the back of the garden, which was at the sharp point of the property. Mrs. Bolotenko happened to be there and helped the brothers over the fence and up towards her house. Jake saw the look of concern on her face, her strong arms lifting him up, her apron wiping the blood away, and heard her words of compassion: "Bidny chlopchik, bidny chlopchik," Poor little boy, poor little boy.

"What is fight about?" Bokotenko stood over Jake, hands on his hips.

"They don't like us Jews."

"So fight them bastards better. Why you Jews no fight better? Same in Czernovitsi, where I come from. Fight them shits. Fight!"

"Yeah…"

"Look. In Palestine Jews fight good. They fight damn British and Arabs. Take lesson from your brothers there."

"Hey. You bleeding lots, boychik. Holy Mother of God, you bleeding so much. *Bidny Chlopchik*."

"Bastards. I seeum. I killum."

"Fascistas. Banderistas."

"I remember such bastards."

"Jesus, Mary, Joseph, you bleeding, still, too much, boy. We go now in hospital fast. Bidny Chlopchik."

"My God. My God. Bidny Chlopchik."

THE COLD ROOM

"Murderers! Killers! Assassins!"

Rabbi Charloff was addressing the Hebrew School class, his six foot-two frame blocking the late afternoon light from the single window over the room.

"Murderers! You killed Mr. Heller."

"Murderers!"

"But you won't kill me!"

Mr. Chaim Heller, the former teacher, had died of pneumonia about six months earlier, as a direct result—so it was said—of being tormented by the five rowdies: Brahm Nyman, Aaron Weidman, Poodgie Silverman, Melvin Kivenko, and Teddie Noble. They had run out of class after being rebuked for making loud synchronized bathroom and barnyard noises.

Mr. Heller, a small, frail young man, followed, trying to round them up, but after chasing them down several blocks through the deep slush along Albion Street, he returned to class with wet feet, steamed-up glasses, and loud wheezing. His death in hospital occurred six days later; his family came from Toronto to claim the body and he was buried there the next day.

Judgement came down swiftly.

"They killed him, the little bastards," Isaac Ravnitzky announced to the small assembly of Colborne Street storekeepers and junk dealers over cokes, coffee, and donuts at Greco's Grill. "The little shits, they oughta be whipped."

"Such a nice young man, Mr. Heller," Boris Israel Tabachnik offered. "I liked him, he knew some Talmud."

"Murder it was. Murder!" said "Max Weisz.

"Terrible!" Renkle harrumped. "According to the law and the constitution…"

"Problem is we'll never get another teacher to come here," said Ravnitzky.

Several months later, however, 'Rabbi' Charloff arrived at the CNR station, his black suit matching the colour of his leather grips, one in each hand, as he stepped forward, unsmiling, to the welcoming committee of Renkle, Ravnitsky, and Tabachnik. They took him to Renkle's for a meal, which he ate in silence, then to his rooms, where he remained for several days awaiting his first meeting with the Hebrew School class.

"Well" observed Tabachnik, "it's the best we can do right now. I could not find out much about his background, except that he comes from Warsaw via Palestine, where he was wanted by the British for suspected activities with the Irgun."

"Yeah, well he's like a lot of men circulating around. Not rabbis at all, but qualified to teach our kids the basics until bar mitzah and then … and he can layen (read) the Torah on Shabbos and schecht (perform ritual slaughter). So that's all we need."

Weisz, speaking now, had been hiring a succession of these 'rabbis' for over twenty years. But acquainted only with primitive and often brutal shtetl teaching methods, neither he nor his committee members were in a position to urge the new hire be an adherent of progressive educational practices. Thus they would not have objected at all to Charloff's opening remarks to the class on his first day.

"Murderers! Murderers! You killed Mr. Heller! But you won't kill me! … I'll kill you! All of you!"

Thereby informed of their fate, the eight year olds like Jake Tabachnik shuddered in their seats, fearing the ways in which they would be done in: fire, strangulation, drowning, beheading, stabbing, or other punishments listed in the Yom Kippur liturgy.

Rabbi Charloff was not finished, however. His excoriations were now directed at the specific culprits in the Heller case.

"I'll break your bones Kivenko, Silverman, Nyman, Weidman, Noble!"

Then lapsing into voluble Warsaw street Yiddish, he named the limbs he would address in his coming orthopedic rampage: "Ichn dir brechen alle beiner, die hent, die feis, und die kopp!" (I'll break all your bones, hands, feet, head), finishing with several blood-curdling curses that elicited dread.

Need one mention that Brantford was not yet acquainted with progressive educational methods?

They shrank even lower in their seats.

Having momentarily exhausted his repertoire of damnation, Charloff turned to the Prayer Book, which he opened at the "Shema," the prayer announcing God's majesty, the recitation of which is required of the Jew immediately before his death. He turned to the fated five.

"Killer Kivenko, read!"

"Shhmaa...! Amm...! Ohhh...!" Kivenko sputtered, his face rapidly reddening as Charloff's massive hand tightened on his throat.

"Criminal Weidman, continue!"

"Shma Yis ... Ow! Oooh! Oy!" This from his suddenly acquired new position on the floor cowering under Charloff's raised fists.

The next victim was identified as "Assassin" and was addressed to Poodgie Silverman, a fat mama's boy, whose left arm Charloff was twisting into an unnatural state. An arc of screaming erupted that reached a remarkably high octave.

"Continue," Charloff shouted, "Mr. Knoble." The "mister" was a sarcastic honorific reserved for the person Charloff regarded as the arch culprit in the "Heller murder," and the "knoble" a pointed reference to and condemnation of Teddie's strong breath, the result of generous home use of garlic (in Yiddish "knoble"). Hence "Mr. Knoble."

"Shm ... aaa" Charloff's vice-like headlock, possibly modeled on famed Toronto professional wrestler Whipper Billy Watson's infamous disfiguring grip on opponents' skulls, had turned Teddie into a paroxysm of pain, his cries of anguish reaching down to the synagogue below.

"Now, Criminal Nyman." Charloff huffed up his shoulders and stretched his fingers aloft as if preparing for a surgical procedure.

"Sh ... ooo. Oh, Ohm. Oh, migod." Charloff was holding Nyman's foot and had twisted it into an emphatic perpendicular direction so as to allow minimal movement and maximum pain.

This procedure was followed by Charloff's swift propulsion of Nyman towards the door leading to an unused room beside the classroom.

Unheated, this space was known, appropriately enough, as the "Cold Room." Windowless, dark, and smelly, its wallpaper peeling away, its floor was flaked with pieces of plaster that had fallen from a badly cracked ceiling. The joists above showed through as more plaster hung down ominously. This was Charloff's ultimate punishment chamber. Here the convict had to endure the cold and stand or sit on the floor for the duration of the class. Moreover, the door that Charloff held open and slammed against the evictee's back as he was part way through the entrance, was hooked. Thus, there was no access to the bathroom.

Having been catapulted onto the floor of the Cold Room, Nyman considered his options. A tough, athletic, and defiant twelve year old, he felt that he had a few.

Recovering from the Rabbi's assault, he cased the room, especially the ceiling. He could see the laths above the cracked plaster and the joists just wide enough apart for a person his size to fit between them. Nyman climbed onto a rickety table sitting in the room and threw his belt over a joist, then pulled himself up into the opening, into the attic. It was really cold in there. But there were possibilities! Escape was one of them. Another was mischief, because the attic extended over the entire second floor – including the classroom.

Nyman moved stealthily over top of Rabbi Charloff. The tables were about to turn.

"Murder Incorporated!" Charloff was screaming to the entire class, including the eight year olds.

"Gangsters, all of you!"

Next there followed his forecast for their imminent doom with a repetition of the complete inventory of the damage he would inflict, limb by limb, bone by bone, and tooth by tooth. "Ichn dir brechen…"

"Umpt, umpt, umpt…." A sudden hammering from above had detached a sizeable lump of plaster that crashed onto the floor, distributing fragments and dust across the desks and flaking Charloff's hair and shoulders with a patina of white particles.

The whole class fled from their seats and huddled in a corner.

"Charloff, you bastard!" Brahm's face could be seen above the shattering ceiling.

"Umpt, umpt umpt…." Another piece of plaster came down.

"Shithead!" Brahm was fuming still and more plaster fell.

"I'll get you!" Charloff yelled and rushed into the Cold Room. When they reached him in there he was already halfway up through the hole, struggling to get through and into the attic. But he was stuck there. Stuck!

Brahm, meanwhile, had lowered himself down into the classroom. He moved quickly to the door of the Cold Room, motioned the class to get out, and locked the door, thus sealing Rabbi Charloff inside. And as they all ran down the stairs into the winter slush on Albion Street, they could hear him shouting:

"You won't kill me! *You won't kill me!*"

HARPO THE GREAT

N o, No, No! Not one of the famous Marx brothers.
Donald Angus Sutherland Harp. He was the sole son of
Angus John, a mechanic at the Cockshutt Plow factory who had
volunteered for R.C.E.M.E (the Royal Canadian Electrical and
Mechanical Engineers) at the start of the Second World War, and
who had gone overseas in 1940. In the interim, Donald, who got
to be known as Harpo, had aged from nine to thirteen and had
become the scourge of a part of the Terrace Hill semi-rural, down-
market neighbourhood that had sprung up after about 1900 on the
northern edge of Brantford.

Come late summer, no fruit tree off the streets or back alleys was
safe from Harpo's late night harvesting, which resulted in sizeable
bounties of apples, pears, peaches, plums, apricots, and cherries
for his pals, which included the Tabachnik brothers.

No back garden was safe from Harpo's uninvited collecting
of the tomatoes, peas, beans, onions, beets, and other legumes
that the householders had laboriously cultivated all spring and
summer. These items were consumed late at night in Harpo's backyard, washed down with Coca Cola or beer stolen from the family
ice box, or redistributed to friends around the neighbourhood to
build alliances in the unceasing gang or club rivalries among the
local eleven to thirteen year old boys, many of whose dads or older
brothers were also in the Forces serving overseas.

This seasonal theft was only a minor neighbourhood nuisance
compared with Harpo's escapades on Halloween, really the two-
week season before and after that fall event, which preceded the

celebration of all the Christian saints the following day. Collecting candy apples, fudge, popcorn, chocolate bars, and other teeth-rotting goodies was tame stuff to him and his crew, which, in addition to the Tabachniks, included a few others (whose full names—all of them now prominent citizens—are best not be listed, for fear of reprisals). In the week before the October 31st event, they moved through neighbourhood streets like raiders of the Golden Horde. Outhouses were overturned—this required special force and great care—especially those belonging to the families of Harpo's enemies at school and in the area.

Clotheslines were cut, even the wire ones, with special clippers removed from the family toolbox. Garbage cans were overturned and their contents strewn across lawns and sidewalks. For the perpetrators' further amusement, the empty cans were tied to the back bumpers of buses stopped at street corners. As the buses started up again, the clattering noise supplied enormous amusement—until the enraged driver stopped, untied the cans, and sometimes chased the perpetrators down the street while yelling obscenities and threatening dire punishments. House and car windows were soaped with the greatest of care, requiring householders and drivers hours of work to obtain enough clarity to be able to get on with the next day's work.

The perps were never caught or punished for their late evening excursions into mayhem, destruction, and theft. They were too fast on their feet and too knowledgeable of the escape routes across backyards and empty lots, into deep foliage alongside back gardens, over fences, down alleyways, over rooftops of sheds and barns, into broken-down silos, up old ladders, through vacant summer kitchens, across verandahs, and up trees.

This was a very modest working-class neighbourhood, where many houses had been built and equipped by occupants who worked at one of the local factories: Cockshutt Plow, Massey Harris Farm Equipment, Brantford Coach and Body Works, Waterous Engineering, or the many small iron and steel shops that dotted the city's industrial quarter, at this time shifting over to the production of components for armaments.

All the while, Harpo's mother, Heather, an immigrant from Glasgow and a real "looker," seemed oblivious to her son's penchant for mayhem. She must have known what was going on, but she never scolded. In fact, when the crew foregathered at their house, located just down the street from Graham Bell School and Shenstone Baptist Church, she made them welcome by offering sandwiches, cake, cookies, pop, and whatever other goodies were at hand. And if she was out, she left the prepared food for them in the ice box.

When at home, Heather seemed to be reading all the time, mostly from the books that arrived regularly from the Book-of-the-Month Club; there were so many of them that her bookshelves overflowed and she stacked the surplus in neat piles beside the console radio. When Harpo's pals entered the house, she'd smile, call out their names for her son to hear, ask after families, and return to her reading while chain-smoking Sweet Caps. As they left, she'd lift her head and wish them well with an "off you go lads" or a "not too late now."

At school and out on the streets Harpo let it be known that he did not brook challenges to his neighbourhood hegemony. Recognized as one of the toughest fighters around, he had a powerful right hook capable of inflicting heavy damage to challengers' faces; thus he commanded considerable respect. Most guys refrained from openly insulting him or members of his crew but, when such violations occurred, and when the balance of power required it, Harpo waded in fists flying. His main opponents were the Pickett brothers, Tom and Henry, who lived up by the United Church, and whose gang included members of the Sergeant clan. In the late summer of 1944, the Picketts began building a clubhouse behind an old barn on their property. This bothered Harpo deeply, and he regarded it as a provocation. And for weeks he talked about little else.

Until two weeks before Halloween—and on the eve of Yom Kippur, just as the Tabachniks were going to shul for Kol Nidre—Harpo turned up at their house looking grim and determined.

"We're gonna wreck the Picketts' clubhouse tonight," he said.

"Not tonight, Harpo. Jewish holiday."

"Yeah? Which One?"

"Yom Kippur. Day of Atonement."

"You guys! 'The People of The Book,' my mom always says. She's Presbyterian."

"Let's wait till Thursday," Jake said. The family was waiting patiently. They liked Harpo.

"OK. My house after dark."

Around nine that night, the crew foregathered at Harpo's: Doug M., Brian H., Don C., and the two Tabachniks. They were ready for action. Over Cokes, cookies and stolen beer, their leader laid out his plan of attack. He first explained that he had arranged with some of his allies to start a fight with the Sergeants in order to draw the Picketts away from their house. Then he gave them their assignments.

Turning to Jake, he said: "You and your brother go in over the Zahorek's fence. Doug and Brian, you go in behind the church yard." This was a heavily treed copse with thick underbrush at the edge of an open field bordering the Picketts' place. "Don, you and I will go in through the Pellegrinis' yard. Let's be very careful not to disturb their flower garden. When we get into the Pickett place, meet up behind the west end of their barn and stay quiet until I deal with their dogs. I've got some meat for them."

"And then what?" asked Doug, who had long harboured reservations about Harpo's zanier escapades.

"Then we smash up the clubhouse, completely, rip it down," Harpo said, as he produced a heavy meat cleaver, two claw hammers, and two large crowbars from underneath a nearby table. He kept the meat cleaver for himself and distributed the other weaponry to the rest of the gang.

Jake got a crowbar.

"Now get the hell out of there," he added.

Just after ten o'clock, they met up behind the barn. Harpo was calm. After carefully placing a bag of meat bones inside the barn and shutting the door after the dogs, he surveyed the scene. All was quiet.

"Now!" he whispered.

Swinging the cleaver he bashed down the clubhouse door and then demolished a small table, several chairs, and a cabinet containing glasses and cups. Meanwhile, the rest of the gang were smashing open the roof and support beams and walls. Within minutes the flimsy structure was in ruins.

"What the hell's going on out there!!" This from a very large adult male silhouetted by the light from the Picketts' back porch.

"Piss on the Picketts!" Harpo yelled, and then whispered to the gang:

"Go!"

They scrambled away, running, heads back, feet pumping, lungs filling, jumping over obstacles, leaping holes and crevices, kicking away debris, weaving and swishing through underbrush, running, running, running. *Running!*

On Harpo's carefully thought-out instructions, they all went directly home and into bed, acting on the possibility of a visit by the police. If they weren't there and still out and about, there'd be a presumption of guilt.

This adventure pointed towards the end of the Harpo gang's depredations. At age fourteen he was becoming more interested in the opposite sex than in battling for supremacy over the Picketts or other challengers.

"There goes last year's joy on wheels," he'd say, after passing a woman pushing a baby carriage.

Or, "Look at them headlights!" while leering at an approaching well-endowed woman.

And he started getting—serious! He began reading what the newspapers, especially the *Brantford Expositor*—dubbed by local wags "The Suppository"—were saying about the war.

By late 1944, his dad's unit was with the Canadian forces fighting in Holland, and Harpo followed letters home while carefully scrutinizing maps in the school library. And the crew was breaking up. Jake's bar mitzvah lessons were about to start, and, when they did, he was drawn into the world of Jewish religious ideas.

In May 1945 the war ended and in the ensuing months the soldiers, including Sergeant Harp, came home. It was just before Halloween, around nine at night. Jake was at his house chatting with Harpo and Heather about changes in their lives when they heard a car door slam. They ran to the front door and saw a burly soldier, lugging a huge army kit bag and carrying an armful of packages, walking up to the porch. Heather screamed and ran to her husband.

But Harpo got there first.

"Dad! Welcome home. I missed you. Dad ... *dad!*"

"I missed you too, Donald. I hear they call you Harpo. I like that ... hey, Harpo, c'mon now, c'mon now. ... Oh Heather my love, my love Heather." She was sobbing uncontrollably. "What's all this fuss and bother? Look at me: not a scratch! Now stop all this. Let's go into the house."

He added. "I'm hungry. Harpo, have you been good?"

"Oh yes, dad, oh yes! I've been good."

FARMERS' DAY

The Spadina Avenue clothing manufacturers' showrooms were alive with the invasion of small town retailers who came to Toronto by car this Wednesday afternoon, as usual, to buy merchandise for their stores. Was 1957 going to be a good year for business? Who could know?

"Hello, how's business in Oshawa?" Boris Israel Tabachnik, just in from Brantford, called out to Sam Glick. He knew him from the old days. Shipmates from Constanza, August 1924.

"Meh. Could be better. We had a bad spring, generally. Don't ask me why. But I sold a few coats. I didn't like the new designs. What's with the lower hemlines? But the customers wanted them, the young ones especially. What do I know?" His arms were outstretched, palms up.

"Same with us. But I couldn't get enough different colours. Sizes too. I can't talk to some of these manufacturers. They don't listen. We give them just small orders. Not like Eaton's, Simpson's, The Bay. 'The farmers' they call us."

"Go to jobbers. They get from Montreal very big supplies every week. Try Shapiro on Richmond Street. You'll find what you want."

"I don't deal with jobbers. They buy leftovers from contractors in the Quebec bushes and I don't buy from their travelers. Contractor bastards. They pay rotten wages to the poor girls there."

"Ah, Boris, don't give me your communistishe bullshit. Like you were on the boat in 1924. This is Canada, not that farkakte, shitty Russia. You wanna make a success here, you look out for your own interests. I go for best price, that's all … manufacturers, contractors, jobbers… I don't care. Have a good winter season."

"OK Sam. See you around. Best wishes to the wife. Children OK?"

"Children? Zolln zai klappen kopp afn vant."

Thus informed that Sam's children were free to bang their heads on a wall, Boris walked away. It was mid-June when orders were being taken for August delivery of winter coats that retailers would put on their front racks for September sales. Sometimes even October.

But now it was hot on "the Avenue," as it was called, really only a five block stretch of that wide street Spadina, which was designed the previous century to be the locale of the city's well-to-do. Now it was the centre of the clothing business, a huge part of the city's economy.

Boris went to Shenkman's Hudson Cloak Company in the Fashion Building to order coats. A highly respected veteran and the acknowledged dean of the Toronto women's coat and cloak trade, Mr. Isaac Shenkman, now in his late eighties, came out to greet an old customer of some thirty years.

"Nu, Tabachnik, how's it in Brantford."

"You know, it's how it is everywhere. 'Business is so bad, even the customers who don't intend to pay aren't buying'."

Boris loved that old saw and Shenkman, who'd probably heard it a thousand times, laughed politely. Tabachnik was a customer who, after all, though only a small-scale buyer, did pay. And on time, too, sometimes even before the invoice was due. And he liked Boris, who sometimes talked of cultural ideas in his rich Odessa Yiddish.

"Let me show you our new line of coats."

"Yes, thank you."

"I like the same basic styles as last year for my older customers, but I'll also order some of the new ones for the special racks, especially misses, the young ones who come in. Three dozen of those, different colours, some smaller sizes."

"Delivery?"

"August 15th, express to you door."

"Price?"

"Same as last year. If you order right now and pay in ten days, I'll pay express charges."

"OK. Three dozen, as I said, and I'll select now from other samples maybe two dozen."

"Fine. I'll write up the order. But I'll need clearance from your bank. Same? Bank of Nova Scotia?"

"Yes. MacCrimmon at the Brantford branch."

Business at Shenkman's completed, Boris proceeded to the Fashion Crest Dress showrooms, waving briefly to the Adler brothers who were just in from Guelph. Tabachnik occasionally bought some of Fashion's lines and had the ready-to-go merchandise from other suppliers delivered there. He would have it all loaded into his car and would carry it back to Brantford, unload it at his store, tag it, and get it up on the racks the next day.

He entered by the side door and noticed two other hometown storekeepers at the front of the showroom—they didn't see him—in deep discussion.

He couldn't help but overhear.

"He can't last. I'll buy him out, twenty cents on the dollar." This from Abe Kivenko, proprietor of Fashion Lane, located just across Colborne Street from Tabachnik.

"I hear he's finished. Can't pay the drafts, even extended." Gershon Reisman, proprietor of Ladies' Lane, located down the street from Tabachnik, was speaking.

"Doesn't run a healthy business."

"Tabachnik's a weakling. Can't survive," Kivenko added.

"So they're talking about me, speculating on my failure," Boris realized. "My friends, Kivenko and Reisman, are discussing me like a piece of furniture, hoping to profit from my failure."

He presented himself loudly, as if just entering the showroom.

"Hello, Abe, Sam. Hello. I didn't know you were in town. Looking for coats today? I just came from Shenkman's; he's got nice lines this year. Have you seen them?"

Kivenko was looking intently out the window.

"Ah … no, not yet."

Freeman shuffled his feet and mumbled something incoherent.

"Have a look. Shenkman makes a good coat, always a quality product I think. The finishing is excellent. A little more money, but worth it."

Silence.

Silence.

"OK boys. I'm off home with these parcels. Gotta pick up meat at Naftoli's and then pastries at Lottman's. Can I get for you anything? No? OK, Regards."

On the way to his car, parked on Richmond Street, he met Jack Dalfen of Acme Dress, a manufacturer of mid-price styles. Boris had bought some of his summer and fall lines. He liked the fabrics, but was not crazy about some of the finishing.

"Hey, Boris, what's with Kivenko."

"Vos mainstu? What do you mean?"

"I hear he's badly behind on his bank drafts. It's known all over the Avenue. Yeah, three months, they say. He's had to mortgage his house to keep his bank manager happy. The Manufacturers Credit Bureau is keeping a close watch."

"Sorry to hear that. I didn't know."

Boris loaded his parcels, went into Kensington Market to buy his kosher meat, bagels, rye bread, and pastries, and headed down Spadina to the Queen E to Hamilton, west along Highway 2 to Brantford; he unloaded his merchandise at the store, and went home.

Next day, he went to his store early. From the safe he took out two thousand dollars in cash.

Then he went across to Kivenko's store.

"Hello Abe, how're things?"

"Meh."

"Problems?"

Abe looked out the window, then at the floor. He blinked several times.

Silence.

"Lately … you know."

"Listen, Abe, here's two thousand dollars. Take it. Maybe it'll help. I don't need it back right away, so...."

"But I thought—"

"Yeah, I know what you thought. I heard you and Reisman in Toronto yesterday. But I want to help you stay in business. Why? You are my friend. Remember the ship from Constanza? Besides, I want you to know that you can't buy me out. But I could, if I wanted to, buy you out."

Silence.

"But as a friend, Abe, I wouldn't do that. Besides, I need you badly for our Thursday night poker games. And besides that, you usually lose."

Silence.

"Ah, Boris, Boris...."

"And sometimes I win...."

AT HEAVEN'S GATE

The bidding started in the usual way. Second-hand furniture dealer Morris Noble, in rumpled suit, fraying shirt, and tattered tie, while peering through smudgy glasses that sagged to one side, began his accustomed nasally chant at the front of the shul:

"T'seinnn dollar Maftir Yoiiinehhh" (Who bids ten dollars for the honour of singing the maftir?), the story of Jonah—a shlemiel if there ever was one—and the whale, from the final prayers that end Yom Kippur.

"T'seinnn dollar Maftir Yoiiinehh," he repeated.

By selling off honours such as calls to the Torah, or this recitation of the maftir on the High Holy days, the congregation was able to add enough revenue to its meagre coffers to maintain the old ramshackle shul and pay the shoichet (teacher) who carried the title of rabbi, but whose real job was to serve as "killer" of chickens for local Jewish consumption and teacher in the Hebrew school. As the final bid was confirmed by Joe's slap on the bima's railing, the shul treasurer, Moishe Ladovsky, quickly entered a numbered slip in his small box file to remind himself to send out a bill the moment the holiday ended.

But this commerce was vital not only for the shul's finances; it was also an important bellweather of the monetary status and ostentatious spending capacity of the town's Jews, few of whom believed in being quiet when they gave away money. It was not enough that such generosity was noticed by the Almighty himself—who, of course, sees all and, on this holiest of holy days, would instruct his heavenly hosts to record the deed in the celestial ledgers and, possibly, stave off any "evil decrees" against them.

No. No. The whole town had to know that Moishe, Shimon, Sam, and Max, the town g'virim—well-to-do scrap or shoddy dealers, or successful downtown merchants—could afford fifty, seventy-five, or a hundred dollars (substantial sums in the 1940s) to buy the most important honours like Maftir Yoineh, which is chanted just before the Gates of Heaven are believed to be closed and celestial judgements are sealed on everyone's fate in the new year, i.e., who would live and who would die, who by stoning, who by strangling, who by fire, who by drowning, and so on, as is threatened in the prayer book.

The auction served the purpose, then, of showing the town who was who right there in front of men, women, and children assembled—while exchanging gossip and appraising everyone else's attire—to beg the Lord for another year of life, health, livelihood, and peace while averting "the evil decree" which the Almighty might have had in mind for them.

Now on this Yom Kippur day 1945, corresponding to the year 5706, Brantford's Jews were about to witness the honours auction of all auctions. Morris Noble had intoned the signal for the bidding to begin—and soon it did. As far back as anyone could remember, Maftir Yoineh had gone to male members of the Mintz clan, well-off dealers in shoddy, now represented by two forty-something brothers, Charlie and Al, burly guys with quick tempers, uncouth speech, and heavy fists. Traditionally, one of them began the bidding, and now Charlie, the elder, smilingly offered twenty-five dollars, confident that he would win, as he always did, at the usual knockdown final price of between eighty and a hundred dollars.

Morris slowly repeated the bid: "Finf und tsvantsig dollar Maftir Yoineh; finf und tsvantsig dollar Maftir Yoineh." And waited.

"Fifty dollar!" Moishe Meltzer, a junk dealer enriched by the wartime inflation in the price of metals, entered the contest in hostile fashion. By doubling Mintz's offer, he was showing serious money quickly, not allowing the usual five or ten dollar increments that let some of the smaller fry momentarily stay in the game, knowing that Mintz would soon outbid them.

The auctioneer, startled now, loudly intoned: "*Fuftsiggg* dollar Maftir Yoinehhh, *Fuftsiggg* dollar Maftir Yoinehhh."

Meltzer, a relative newcomer, was making a statement. He now had as much, or more, money than the Mintz brothers and was determined to put them down—and raise himself up—in public esteem by outbidding them. He and his brother, though suddenly enriched, had not enjoyed a good reputation in recent years. The scrap business was renowned for shady practices, including alleged outright theft of competitors' goods, and Meltzer's name was associated—perhaps wrongly—with some of the worst. Local wags speculated that guilty consciences explained the loudness and fervour of the Meltzers' davening on this holy day, their strict religiosity year round, and the huge talesim with which they were covering, as it were, their alleged multitudinous misdemeanours.

Such was the malicious gossip, lashon ha'rah, which, though frequently condemned by the rabbi, nevertheless constituted the very substance of communal discourse.

Battle was now joined and the Mintzes, who hated such chutz-pah, especially from the likes of the Meltzers, immediately raised their bid to seventy-five dollars, Meltzer countering instanta-neously with one hundred.

There was now a pause—a very pregnant one.

Auctioneer Noble, his gray shirt darkening and glistening, and his glasses near flying off his nose as he swiveled nervously from looking at one side of the shul to the other, sputtered and shook. The congregation was captivated and enormously amused at the rivalry of the two families. Renkle, the shul president, chortled under his breath as he contemplated the higher revenue that the rivalry would bring in. Meanwhile, Falia Strenkhovsky, the self-appointed community maven on all things religious, privately fumed over this violation of Yom Kippur propriety.

What would the Mintzes do now that Meltzer had offered one hundred dollars, the highest knockdown price Maftir Yoineh had ever fetched?

"Screw them," Charlie muttered loudly to his brother, Al, whose own recent business past included (it was widely rumoured) running a low-grade downtown establishment frequented mainly by soldiers from the nearby Army base housing hundreds of the hated Zombies, the term widely applied to army conscripts who lawfully refused to volunteer for general service. Al nodded his approval.

"A hundred and fifty," Charlie shouted.

Meltzer immediately countered with two hundred.

The congregation gasped.

The rabbi lifted his eyes to heaven. "Gottenu," he muttered, disgusted.

For Morris Noble and everyone else this was no auction: it was a public row between the two families and it was more than he could handle. He grew red and began to sweat. His glasses dipped to the very end of his nose and he held onto the rail of the bima looking to Renkle for help. Renkle was no stranger to trouble in the town.

"Enough!" he shouted.

For a brief moment the shul fell silent. Even the children went quiet. But the Mintz brothers were already on their feet, ignoring Renkel and hurling defiance at the Meltzers. "Two hundred and fifty, you chazerim!" Al screamed and shook his fist.

Such language in shul—and on Yom Kippur. (Was the Almighty listening?)

All the while, the women, who sat at the back behind a curtain, had not been involved in this contretemps, although comments, laughs, and winks were being exchanged. The contenders' wives sat intensely tight-lipped, while eyeing their embattled husbands with mounting disdain.

"For this idiocy we left Europe," Esther Meltzer mordantly observed finally, for all to hear. She then marched up through the men's section and confronted her husband:

"Are you a complete fool?" she screamed. To which her husband had no answer.

"Let them have their Maftir Yoineh. Stop now or I will bid against *you*." She took off her diamond ring—worth, it was commonly agreed, a good few hundred dollars—and held it up in front of her husband's face: "With *this*," she said, "I'll bid *this*! And I'll give the maftir to the Mintzes, as a gift. How would you like *that*?"

Silence.

And the auction ended right then and there. The Mintzes won and the shul was a little bit richer than it usually was from these annual contests. But the auctions were never the same again and were abandoned not long afterwards for more dignified—but far less amusing—proceedings. In any event, Morris Noble was not able to continue, so flustered was he by the day's drama. The Mintzes were so peeved at having to pay two and a half or three times more for what they got that they let it be known they wouldn't bid again, while Meltzer, who had dared to upset tradition, had been humiliated in front of the whole congregation by his very own wife.

But on this occasion the rabbi resumed prayers, all the more fervently for the day's crass display, while the protagonists glared at each other. Meanwhile, the gates of Heaven remained open.

RAVNITZKY'S REVENGE

"**M**amzerim! Sonsofbitches! Besteds!"

When Isaac Ravnitzky got to swearing, language was no barrier. In Yiddish, Russian, Polish, Ukrainian, Georgian, Kazakh, Chechen, and pidgin English, he was widely known to be as foul-mouthed as a Navy rating, and he was so now, as he stewed in his junkyard office on Grand Trunk Street near the CNR repair shops.

"Sonsabitches! Cholerias! Ganovim! Shits!" he screamed.

Ravnitzky was used to the tricks of the trade. But he had never seen this! Somehow, the three tons of steel scrap he had shipped out that morning weighed only two and three quarters tons on the scales at Goldblatt's yard near the Stelco mill in Hamilton, so he had been informed by his driver, and the receipt now sat on his desk.

"A yor aff zey! Zoln zey brennen!" His lexicon of foulness momentarily at an end, he was resorting to curses, a talent for which he was widely known. "In der erd zoln zey vaksn!" which advised evil days for all cursees.

This was followed by foul threats against nameless enemies. "When I find out, I'll sue de bukkers!" And then more swearing, his natural verbal habitat: "Ganovim! Oisvorfs! Chazerim! Blady!"

This wasn't the first time Ravnitzky's shipments to Hamilton scrap dealers had been a quarter, even a half, ton short. Almost every other truck load going out at, say, three tons on his scales weighed in at two and a half or three quarter tons on arrival in Hamilton.

And he had complained. Oy, had he complained! He had gone directly to Goldblatt himself, demanding to know "what the hell." Goldblatt had shown him up-to-date government inspectors' reports certifying the correctness of his scales. In fact, both Goldblatt and his competitors were widely known in the trade as scrupulously honest on weights, both with their suppliers, such as Ravnitzky, and with their customers, like Stelco and Dofasco, whose giant mills engorged thousands of tons of the metallic detritus trucked or railroaded in from around southern Ontario.

So what was the problem? Ravnitsky had his own scales checked and rechecked, so there was nothing amiss at his yard. And if there was a minor glitch, surely it wouldn't account for a quarter or half ton shortfall per load.

No. The problem lay elsewhere. But where? "Ribboinoi shel oylem, give me an answer," he moaned. Where could a quarter ton of shavings, cuttings, and other bits and pieces of cars, farm machinery, and other items disappear to? Does the devil himself swoop down on a loaded truck on the road to Hamilton and make a meal of steel scrap? Does the shadowy Lillith, the eternal mischief-maker, mockingly turn Ravnitzky's junk into thin air? Is some evil golem making its presence known and sending him a message? Or is this, he wondered, a sign, a warning possibly, from the Almighty himself?

Ravnitzky, his swearing now exhausted, ruminated on such matters while gazing gloomily out of the window into his vast yard filled with piles of metals, bottles, and cardboard. Washing machines and bathtubs commingled there with car engines and door panels, pipes, angle iron, steel cuttings and shavings—the offscourings of modern industrialism soon to be melted down in giant open hearth furnaces into new steel for tanks and cannons. And airplanes.

Airplanes! Images of his son, Fred, a Royal Canadian Air Force bomb aimer, who languished in a German prisoner of war camp, momentarily flashed before him.

But the immediate question was—who the hell was stealing his steel? If it wasn't the spirits, who was it?

He had never had this problem. Mitro Zahoryk, his yard manager for decades, had seen to the loading of trucks, the weights carefully noted in the office ledger. The trucks then set off up the highway to Hamilton. But when they arrived, it was another story.

So, on the way ... on the way ... Ravnitzsky thought slowly. On the way ... a quarter ton—disappears.

He knew what he had to do.

Next day, driving a borrowed car, he followed his heavily-laden Studebaker four-ton truck down the road.

Out of the city it went, east towards Hamilton, following the normal route to the highway. Once there, the driver drove carefully and well within the fifty mile an hour speed limit along Highway 2. But, at Alberton, he turned off to the right onto County Road 33 (well-known among Brantford Collegiate boys for the whorehouse down an unmarked lane).

"What's he doing? Where is he going?" Ravnitzky wondered as he followed along.

"Why is he stopping here? And pulling off behind that barn?"

"He's getting out of the cab. He's climbing up onto the back of the truck."

"My scrap, he's throwing out. Oy."

"Now he's stopped. Getting back into the truck."

Ravnitzky ducked as the truck passed, veered left onto the main road, and proceeded east toward Hamilton. He then rose in his seat to get a good look at the scene behind the barn. There was a substantial amount of scrap scattered about, around two and a half to three tons, he guessed.

"Who's this?" Another truck, this one empty, had arrived. He recognized the driver. It was Yvan Perozak, one of Meltzer's men.

So that was it! His competitor, Moishe Meltzer had pre-arranged the drop-off and was taking the scrap and selling it as his own in Hamilton.

Profanities now flowed from Ravnitzky's mouth like Seagram's VO at a bar mitzvah. But what to do?

The answer was obvious: a bet din (court) in front of Rabbi Levine, known locally as the Hamiltoner Rebbe, a venerable and frail little man of experience, wisdom, and patience for the failings and foibles of his people. In his forty years as rabbi he had heard cases without end, afterwards dispensing judgements with deep sighs, concerning marital problems, business disputes, and wounded vanities. He had listened for years to countless tales of infidelities, as wives poured out their overflowing hearts about their wayward husbands' affairs with salesgirls and secretaries; occasionally husbands brought him stories of wives being "visited" by other men. After listening to such anguish, the Rabbi tried to find ways of bringing complainants back to marital fidelity and peaceful (more or less) domestic life. And also bring warring business partners to reconciliation. He healed bruised egos.

"Zoll zeyn sholem bayis" (let there be peace in the home), he would always admonish, knowing that this advice was not enough to overcome the endless possibilities of the corruption of the flesh among his flock in this "treife medinah," this unholy country.

"Ribboinoi shel oylem, Master of the Universe," he would silently intone. "Oy, ribboinoi shel oylem." Sometimes the foibles of his people were almost too much for him to bear.

On the appointed day for the bet din, the venerable Rabbi Levine, his cane resting against his knee, leaned over the table in his book-filled study:

"Reb Ravnitzky, state your case."

"Meltzer here has cheated me out of over seven hundred dollars for several years by stealing my scrap, which I send by truck to Goldblatt's. I have evidence."

"Reb Meltzer, how do you answer?"

"I deny everything."

A long and noisy process ensued, during which Ravnitzky's evidence—truck drivers' testimony, a stack of weigh bills, and photographs—persuaded the Rabbi that the charges were well-founded.

Turning to Meltzer he said:

"Reb Meltzer, you must pay back Reb Ravnitzky the money you stole from him."

Silence.

Ravnitzky got to his feet: "Rabbi, I don't want the money back. I want only Meltzer should let his daughter marry my son, Freddy, when he comes home from the war." … "God willing." He thought it prudent to add that for the Rabbi.

"Like hell! She's not going to marry him. He joined up the Air Force, the fool. And what happened? He's a prisoner of war in Germany writing letters to my Chana. But who knows what condition he'll come home back. No. I'm looking for a better shidduch (marriage) for her."

The Rabbi looked at Meltzer and then at Ravnitzky.

"Bring the girl next week, Wednesday, one o'clock in the afternoon."

The following week, the court reassembled.

"What is your name?" Rabbi Levine asked.

"Helen Meltzer."

"Your Jewish name?"

"Chana."

"Chana. You wish to marry the boy Ravnitzky when, God willing, he returns from the war?"

"Oh yes."

"Yes? You are sure?"

"Yes, yes."

"How old are you. And what is your occupation?"

"Nineteen. I am a student in biology at McMaster University."

The Rabbi turned to Meltzer.

"Reb Meltzer. You will publicly announce in shul next Shabbos that you bless this shidduch and promise that, when the boy returns, you will make them a wedding. You will also provide a dowry of seven hundred dollars. In Ravnizky's honour you will also make a kiddush lunch in shul next Shabbos and give a donation to charity of one hundred dollars."

"I will not do any of this Rabbi."

"So then Ravnitzky goes to the police. You want to stand trial on criminal charges?"

Silence.

Silence.

"I want an answer now, Reb Meltzer!"

Silence.

"What is your answer?"

"Seven hundred dollars?"

"That's how much you stole!"

"And a kiddush for Ravnitzky?"

"I insist! Otherwise the police will visit you."

Meltzer was silent while he considered the probability of standing in front of "the Major," whose stare from the bench could freeze water.

"Your answer!"

"All right … All right."

"Fine." The Rabbi said and turned to Ravnitzky.

"Reb Ravnitzky, you will give something in return."

"*I* should give? He stole from *me*."

"Your son, God willing, soon will marry a fine girl. To show appreciation, you will make a gift to the couple of five hundred dollars. You will also put a large plaque in the shul. The plaque will consist of the Ten Commandments—which, as you know, prohibits bad language—and at the bottom a dedication from you in honour of Reb Meltzer.

"And if I don't?"

"Then I wash my hands of all this and you will have to make your case in court."

Silence.

More silence.

"What's your answer?"

Ravnitzky sighed, then nodded.

The rabbi got up and shuffled out of the room. The bet din was over.

Meltzer glared at Ravnitsky. Ravnitzky smiled and glared back.

"NAKED WOMEN IN SHUL"

As far as anyone could figure, Maxie Wexler did not do anything particular in town. Sometimes he helped out in the family tailoring shop selling two dollar shirts and twenty-five cent ties, while his father made alterations on a suit in the back room. Maxie's brother, David, had been killed in a training accident while on duty with the Royal Canadian Air Force in 1941. Maxie, then a medical student at the University of Western Ontario, suddenly lost interest in his studies, dropped out, and returned to town, where he just hung around. He had an artistic bent and was active in the shul's cultural life, mainly in directing the Hanukah and Purim plays that allowed him lots of scope.

Among Maxie's many interests was modern dance, and he decided one day to offer classes in which he would instruct the community's younger women in the art of ballet. And so, after the usual communication system—Murafsky's grocery store, Greco's Grill, the Albion Street "Yiddishn Gass," and the telephone—had been fully employed, about fifteen women assembled in the shul's social hall one winter evening for their first lesson.

Women often gathered in the shul, mostly to cook for various community functions. No problem there. The new building, Beit Baruch (in memory of Billy Bucavetsky, who was killed in action in 1943 while serving with the RCAF), which had opened in 1947 with a one-block parade down Albion Street from the old shul, sported handsome facilities, including an up-to-date kitchen just for the women.

But this time there was a problem: the way they were dressed—or should one say, undressed. Maxie, it seems, had instructed them to bring exercise attire; consequently, they had all disrobed down to shorts and short sleeves, and in several cases bathing suits. The class began with Maxie, similarly clothed, going through the demonstrations of basic exercises and preliminary steps while one of the ladies played the piano.

How did Jake know all of this, you may ask? Because he was in the building at the time, studying in a downstairs classroom with Rabbi Gelder and two other pupils a tractate of the Talmud, Baba Metziah, which deals with lost and found articles and begins (as he remembered it, from the Aramaic): "Shnayim ochazim b'talit. Zeh omer hakol sheli,v'zeh over hakol sheli," "Two individuals find a tallit (lying in the street). One of them says 'it all belongs to me' and the other, confrontationally, says the same."

Rabbi Gelder, employing traditional gestures, with his right elbow raised, fist clenched, and thumb outstretched but dipping towards the book, was just about to begin the explanation of the ensuing passage, which provides the answer to this eternal Jewish juridical dilemma, when from up above in the social hall there came the sounds of the *pas de deux* from Swan Lake. The rabbi stopped in mid-sentence and looked up from the text. As the music continued, the class heard a series of thumping sounds, as if a dozen basketballs were being dropped onto the floor above. Then again more thumps!

"What's happening up there?" the Rabbi said. "Benny, go have a look," he nodded to Ben Weidman; and to the rest of the class, "We will continue now." So they went back to the issue of who would keep the newly found tallit. "Explain to me now the problem here," said the Rabbi, looking at Jake. Jake was about to say that there should not be a problem if the two finders would agree to take half the value of the tallis each—a simplistic answer, to be sure—when a red-faced Benny burst into the room shouting "Rabbi! There are women in shorts and bathing suits dancing around up there!"

There are moments that are sometimes described as "pregnant" and others as "significant," "rich," "sacred," or "precious." The seconds that followed were none of the above: they were utterly overwhelming. The boys were thunderstruck—and, at age fifteen, pruriently curious.

In the shul, women in shorts and bathing suits? In the *shul*?!

The Rabbi's face turned red, then black. "What did you say?" he queried.

"Rabbi, I saw Mrs. Brown, Mrs. Resnick, and—"

"Stop with the names!" he screamed. "What's happening?"

"They are dancing in shorts and bathing suits," said Benny.

Another silence followed, this one very pregnant.

"Go home now," mumbled the Rabbi, his face a bright crimson. He stumbled to his feet, threw on his coat, and pushed his pupils towards the door. Though curious—and not about the answer to the Talmud problem—they did as he said, but slowly.

That was not the end of the affair. The next Shabbat, after morning services ended, all the men were discussing what had happened that night in the social hall. Expressing outrage at the violation of their religious space (but, no doubt, thinking their private thoughts), they chattered over their schmaltz herring and Seagrams 83 about the nakete frauen in shul, the naked women in the shul. Jake's grandfather repeated the phrase several times to himself as they walked home together.

Rabbi Gelder put an immediate stop to these goings-on by demanding that the president, Louis Renkle, intervene—or else! Renkle was forced to comply, though privately, he might have been far from outraged. Maxie was given his walking papers from shul activities and the women were told to dance, if they must, any-where but there.

Such a scandal.

But it was nothing compared to the news circulating around town that one of the women present was Malka—the Rabbi's own wife.

THE COLLECTOR

"Look at him." This from Moe Schweitzer, local pool hall owner responding to an appeal for charity.

Moe was speaking about Boris Israel Tabachnik, local Zionist leader, fundraiser, organizing galvanizer of the Brantford Jewish community, busybody, activist, Congress representative—and collector.

"Who the hell asked you to go collecting money?"

"We've gotta do it, Moe. The refugees need help. We need money to help them. C'mon Moe, I need your cheque."

"Look at him," repeated Moe, now addressing a couple of his pals shooting pool.

Boris suddenly grabbed Schweitzer's neck and squeezed hard and long enough to choke him until tears filled Moe's eyes.

"Talk to me like that again and I'll break some of your teeth, you wormy little shit." This warning was delivered in fragrant Odessa street Yiddish.

Boris then presented himself to very well-to-do junk dealers, who were less contemptuous, but not generous.

"One hundred dollars, take it or leave it."

"I'll take it. Thank you." Boris gritted his teeth and forced a smile. These bastards in a thieving business had only recently bought themselves new homes, flashy suits, Buicks, garish furniture, minks for their wives, and expensive holidays.

And they're giving a mere one hundred dollars to help Holocaust survivors, he thought to himself. They should choke on their shitty money.

He moved on. A poor junk collector offered forty in one and two-dollar bills. Accepted with a handshake, a warm smile and a hug, Boris, an atheist, wasn't into bestowing blessings. But if he had been, he would have.

Next, Louis Renkle. The community's German was generous.

"Here's a cheque for one thousand dollars, Boris. Maybe it'll help. Oh, by the way, we have to organize a clothing drive for the refugees. Let's meet soon to discuss plans."

On to the next Colborne Street Jew. Max Weisz, also a longtime furniture store proprietor, whose fractured English sent listeners into fits of squelched laughter, like the time he said, before giving a speech: "I've got to check my nuts" (instead of notes). But he was also generous with a cheque, always careful to match his competitor Renkle. Plus an open wallet to anybody in need, including more than one offer to pay university tuition fees if that would prevent a family crisis.

Nachum Nyman was next on the list. He ran a prosperous upscale ladieswear store that dominated his whole block on Colborne Street, this after years of "pioneering" as a drygoods peddler in rural areas nearby. He was a thin chain-smoker who ground his teeth when angry and shouted in shul when upset by glitches in the proceedings. "Here's my cheque, Boris." It too was respectable.

Next, to his own competitors in retail ladieswear, Gershon Reisman, was a short, unhappy man with an unusually hysterical wife and two nervous sons. His cheque for two hundred dollars was also respectable. This was not true of others, however. Kivenko, Boris' close friend, donated a poor fifty, while Yakov Perlman did the same: both were comfortable merchants and could well have afforded more.

Not so some of the petty junk dealers. Israel Granofsky eked out a living with his small truck, making the rounds for castoffs of all kinds. Mr. Rapaport collected, too, but mostly barrels that were stacked up in the yard behind his house down by the CNR station; this made for just modest returns. His wife was a huge lady of saintly spirit and habits: she happily cooked kosher food and brought it up to Jewish hospital and sanatorium patients. She fed numerous waifs and strays who blew into town—con men, drifters, schnorrers—and ended up penniless at her door. The Rapaport family income allowed for only a modest donation, a few dollars, which Boris accepted gracefully.

In fact he accepted nearly all of them, balking only when disgust overtook him on seeing blatant disregard of "responsibility," such as when of a cheque of, say, fifty dollars was offered by a well-to-do family that foreswore no indulgences, even the most posh ones. On these occasions, Boris would either tear up the cheque in front of the donor, saying "Call me when you are prepared to be serious," or, "This is ridiculous, I'm not accepting this from you!" or even "Have you no shame!"

Such tactics were risky, of course. But almost always the chintzy donor would return contrite with a new donation sufficiently increased that Boris took the new cheque without hesitation, fully realizing that he wouldn't get more and that holding out further would be potentially damaging to community stability.

The ultimate community control mechanism for charitable contributions was "the list," a roster of names with amounts contributed. The list was typed, mimeographed, and distributed. Boris made sure that everyone in town got a copy—also that information reached United Jewish Appeal officials in Toronto, which coordinated such fundraising efforts across Ontario. This communication sometimes had salutary side benefits. Some Toronto businessmen were known to refuse to engage further with small-town associates they regarded as holdouts or cheapskates. A local junk dealer, whose listed donation Boris disparaged as unworthy of a man he knew could afford much more, was told by his Toronto associate to "get the hell out of his office." One trucking tycoon publicly threatened, stupidly of course, to blockade the businesses of fellow Jews who weren't donating up to his standards. Rough tactics perhaps, but emotions ran high after the Holocaust. And the survivors needed help.

Most of the time, the pressure was more polite and Boris applied it only where it would likely be effective. Complete holdouts were extremely rare and usually involved people regarded as nutbars of some variety. There were a couple of these in Brantford: one saw himself as a 'citizen of the world' and only 'by accident' a Jew. The other was a poor tailor, Harry Stern, a Holocaust survivor who was so traumatized that he just could not be approached for anything. He had two gold teeth and had repaired German uniforms at Auschwitz before moving to town and setting up a small shop off the main street. Now he repaired old suits long into the night. He smiled blankly at his few customers, and his petite wife, Rina, also a survivor, often peered out nervously from behind the door leading to their living quarters behind the shop. She seldom came to community events and watched over her two skinny children with religious fervour.

Sometimes pressures came from another direction. Boris very reluctantly accepted a twenty dollar cheque from the proprietors of a highly successful business because their son, Sam, had just returned from four RCAF years of duty with Bomber Command, where he had served a total of fifty missions. *Fifty.* Just out of uniform, Sam came over to see Boris and handed him a cheque for an additional two hundred—this out of his demob money—asking if that would be enough for now.

Kids brought in allowances and, most moving of all, some Christians came forward. The Rawdon Street Baptist Church members en masse collected a considerable sum from their working class folk. One elderly woman handed Boris her government pension cheque for $61.50, saying that "the Jews were God's chosen people" and that "Israel must live." Although he tried to refuse this donation because he knew it would undermine the poor woman's actual living conditions, the look on her face made him reconsider, and he accepted. What else could he do? He got into his car crying.

Then there were "the Czechs," farming Jews from the Moravian region of Czechoslovakia who had arrived in 1938 and 1939 to settle on farms in the Brantford area. About a dozen or fifteen families, they were a different breed from the Eastern Europeans. They were mostly cultured people, German-speakers who had arrived with considerable libraries of Goethe, Schiller, and the works of other literary giants. They also brought over records, the large discs available of Bach, Beethoven, Brahms, and of the great bel canto operas by Rossini and Verdi. They knew about art and had visited the Louvre and the Prado, and the Vienna, Rome, and Berlin galleries. Their conversation was filled with the *kultur* of central Europe and their English, while accented, was redolent of insight and commentary on the paintings of Klimt, Kandinski, and Picasso. In a community made up of swearing and sweating junk dealers and jumped-up peddlers from the backwaters of Eastern Europe, "the Czechs" stood out.

But most of them were not susceptible to appeals for funds. Not that they had cash to spare, being farmers. And in that they stood out too, having arrived with a farming background—some with university degrees in agronomy—and an intimate knowledge of advanced techniques in, for example, what they called "permanent pasture," which yielded three or four crops of fodder annually instead of only one or two, giving them a huge advantage in the local dairy industry. They knew what they were doing on their farms.

Boris liked "the Czechs" and thought up good reasons to visit them, sometimes taking his kids along to see the barns and cows. And "the Czechs" liked him, it seems, a Russian Jew with a warm smile, a sharp, inquiring mind, and a good secular education that allowed him to meet them on their own cultural level. They conversed in English, Mr. Abeles' Germanic hues mixing with Boris' Slavic Yiddish tones creating the mellifluous sounds of old Europe in Canadian English in the heart of Ontario. Talk of ideas, writers, politics, and of course "the Jewish question," rebounded among the books and the huge wind-up phonograph player. After an hour or so, Boris thanked the Czech for his donation, and for the tea and buns, and moved on.

Now to the rabbi. Rabbi Gedaliah Gelder had only recently arrived and was barely settled in his house—which was technically not his, as it belonged to the congregation—before being deluged with the problems of his community. Boris' mission here was to enlist the rabbi's endorsement of the campaign in the form of a commitment that he would make in a statement in shul next Shabbos. The rabbi agreed, though not before offering his critical views of the godless ways of the kibbutzniks for free love, children's villages, mixed bathing, and other "scandalous behaviour." Boris listened patiently, then left.

Finally, over to the Strenkhovskys, proprietors of a large business that made industrial cleaners for distribution across the country. The family elder, Falia (or Freddy), who had served at the front in the Russo-Japanese War, was a former rag and bone dealer whose son, Jack, after army service in the 48th Highlanders, had turned the business into a thriving concern, with a plant employing dozens of workers who processed the rags and shoddy into packaged industrial wipes of various qualities.

"Jack, you know why I'm here."

Turning to Falia, Boris said, "Sholom Aleichem," and smiled.

"Here Boris. One thousand dollars."

"Thank you, Jack."

"Tell me, Boris, why you do this collecting of money for these causes? It can't be easy. Why do you do it?"

"I do it for the honour, Jack. For the honour."

AH! GLENDA!

"I don't go out with short guys like you, Jake. You're a twerp, a shrimp."

"Well, Glenda, that's true. But ever heard of small packages and good things?"

"Hmm, I might give you a try. When is that dance and what in hell is the U.N.D.T?"

"It's U.N.T.D., University Naval Training Division."

"Jake, the war's been over for ten years. What's this all about?

"I'll tell you one of these days, but not now. You coming with me or not? This is a one-time offer. It's next month, the 14th, and I gotta buy tickets, which will cost me most of what's in my bank account. So, Glenda: yes or no?"

"Give me till tomorrow. I'll tell you then. Gotta go. See you, Shrimpy. Oh, and did you say something about dinner first?"

"Yeah, I did."

"And can you afford that too?"

"You know what, Glenda, do me a big favour and just say no and I'll spend the evening over at the Battalion Club drinking beer and listening to "Turtle," the vet who's always there, telling me for the fortieth time about the Canadian Army's attacks on the Germans at Passchendaele.

"And have me miss all the fun at the dance?"

"So is that a Yes?"

"Tell you tomorrow. Bye, mon petit twerp."

She flounced off. Jake just loved that flounce as she moved away. And so did lots of other guys around the Junior Common

Room at University College, the hangout of many Jewish students in the 1950s. Glenda was a "dish," a very attractive freckle-faced redhead from a well-off Ottawa Jewish family in the third year of the Honours French programme. Her twin brother, Andrew, was in Engineering Physics and played trumpet in the Lady Godiva Memorial Band. A wild bugger, they said, but brilliant.

Glenda played tennis and Jake would sometimes go over and watch her. Enthralled. They would then go for a drink to UC or to the Battalion Club, a veteran's group on Willcocks Street at the corner of Huron. Beer for Jake and Pinot Noir for her. She would sip it slowly and smoke a Gitane or two.

"Where did you get those? Are they sold here?"

"No. From Émile."

"Émile? … Who's Émile?"

"The new instructor in Eighteenth-Century Lit. He's on leave from the Sorbonne."

"Oh yeah. And where was he during the war? In the *Résistance*, I'll bet, bravely blowing up German troop trains."

"Or moving downed Allied airmen to the Spanish border."

"Or, how's this, Glenda: maybe he served in Pétain's fascist *Milice* who rounded up Jews and shipped them to Auschwitz? Ever thought about that, Glenda?"

"Just shut up, Jake. You're full of shit right now."

Next day she said "Yes, I'd love to." And if there was a financial problem about dinner, she'd treat them both. And she kissed Jake on the cheek before leaving.

Then she flounced off.

That flounce, you had to see it.

Financial problem? Just this: it took almost all of Jake's summer Navy service savings to pay tuition fees and buy books. For digs, he had a cheap room in a house next to the Battalion Club, where he enjoyed their twenty-cent beer while listening to the vets— now geezers—talk about Vimy Ridge, where they'd kicked the Germans' asses and won the day. But for Glenda, Jake would beg, borrow, or steal enough to take her out. Damned if he'd let her pay. He'd sooner eat macaroni for a month than let her do that.

So out they went. With no car, Jake splurged on a taxi to La Chaumière, where they teamed up with some of his U.N.T.D. mates over coq au vin or boeuf bourguignon and consumed several bottles of wine. She drank Chablis and smoked … Gitanes.

Émile again!

At the dance Glenda was giddily superb. Wearing a bright red, sheer, partly see-through dress, over evidently black basics, she was the hit of the night. Her waltz was elegant and subdued. Her fox trot was pert and peppy. Her rhumba was flouncy and sexy. Her samba flowed and weaved. And all through the evening she wouldn't take her eyes off of Jake, the shorty, the shrimp, the twerp. In his arms she glowed, glided, and swooned. Her red hair glistened, her freckles shone, her eyes seduced, and her body shimmied.

And she got noticed.

"Cadet Tabachnik," a well-lubricated Lieutenant inquired. "Who is that gal?"

"Oh, her name's Glenda, Sir. Her brother was a paratrooper and an enforcer for the Soo Greyhounds. He's now facing three charges for attempted murder."

"Oh, oh, I see. Enjoy the evening."

"Thanks, Sir."

"Hey Jake. Who's your gal?" This from a fellow cadet.

"Her name's Glenda. She's a professional judo instructor with a bad temper."

"Wow. Well, she can grab me anytime."

"Yeah. Well, not tonight."

Jake took her home and they embraced longingly. She lived up two flights of stairs over a tailor's shop on Harbord Street. She went up and Jake stayed below, wondering.

On the first landing, she looked down at him and smiled. On the second, she called down: "I need help, shorty. Door's open."

Jake was "ready in all respects"—an appropriate Navy boast—and went up and helped her.

All night long.

They were together a lot after that. Coffee at Nick's, beer at the Battalion Club, corned beef sandwiches at Switzer's and Becker's, meals at Goldenberg's, burgers at Macpherson's lunch counter, and a few times for dinner at La Chaumière. (He let her treat. He had to.)

He'd meet her often after her Eighteenth-Century Lit seminar finished, on late Thursday afternoons, waiting in the UC cloisters in the dark. She'd emerge, usually smoking a Gitane.

And he would usually see Émile, too: fortyish, sporting a Van Dyke, wearing a black beret and a belted coat, and carrying a briefcase with straps. Moving swiftly in the winter darkness.

And smoking a Gitane.

Later that year, Glenda moved in with Émile—in those days a veritable scandal— and she avoided Jake. Whenever he came near, she turned away, red-faced.

Soon after graduation, she moved to Paris with Émile.

Jake never saw her again.

THE TENTH MAN

O f course it was entirely Jake's fault. He should have known what was likely to happen. He had seen this before. So, while innocent, he was really guilty.

Jake, a new history prof working on a book about Montreal, was in Philadelphia on a research trip to an archive that housed the papers of an eminent rabbi who had corresponded during the mid-nineteenth century with a Montrealer of importance in the city's Jewish social and political affairs. He had spent two days going through the collection and that morning finished up by ordering photocopies that would be ready around two o'clock. After lunch he planned to review the rest of the rabbi's letters to see if there were other items of interest. It was Thursday and the archives closed at four. He would then have just enough time to collect his stuff at the hotel and get to the airport for the flight home. Now he was on an extended lunch break walking around the historic Society Hill district, which years before had been the home turf of many of the city's Jews and their synagogues.

And then it happened. Having stopped in front of an imposing old synagogue, he was looking up at the inscription carved in the stone lintel above the entrance: "Rodeph Shalom" (People pursuing Peace). How fitting, he thought, in this city of brotherly love. The cornerstone's Hebrew lettering read 1897.

Jake didn't see him coming, or he would have bolted. But he heard the words and knew right away that he was done for.

"Du bist der tsenter." The man had come right out with it!

The expression literally means "You are the tenth man," but that is not its full historical, cultural, and religious meaning; not by a long shot. Volumes, encyclopedias would be necessary to fully explain it. But I'll be brief:

Ten adult men—post-bar mitzvah, that is—are required for prayer and the reading of the Torah. And since it was Thursday, the Torah was to be read for Mincha, the afternoon prayers. Does anybody know why the quorum is ten and not, say, nine or eleven? No. Jake was a mere historian who scribbled stuff that was of no real account in the big world. So you'll have to go argue with God about this, if you can find him—though Jake often wondered how many people He can listen to.

"Du bist der tsenter," he had pronounced. Once the words have been spoken, any wandering, solitary Jew is … "toast." You have been nabbed, dragooned, and shanghaied into the group awaiting the required number for prayer.

Run away? Sure, with nine elderly men smiling at you because you are making it possible for them to collectively approach God in that hour. Run away? Jake wouldn't dare. If you have been raised on the Canadian cliché that "the Mounties always get their man," then you will perhaps understand that nine Jewish men hoping for a tenth are no less relentless than the Royal Canadian Mounted Police. And when they find "der tsenter," he cannot, dare not, escape.

Guilt beats handcuffs any time.

Jake's captor, a tall, white-haired, portly man supported by a cane in each hand, ushered him into the synagogue and paraded him in front of his friends. And then it began.

"Fun vanen kumt a Yid?" someone said.

This is a trick question. Literally, it means simply "Where does a Jew [you] come from?" But that's not what the interlocutor is really asking. What he wants from you is a full explanation for your presence there. Not just your last point of origin, but also where you were before that, and where your father and mother came from, and where they are now, and what do they do for a living, and, and, and…

Get the point?

A wily academic to the core, Jake began to respond cautiously, economically, sparingly, intending to squelch the expected follow-ups. But a cop's 'third degree' is nothing compared to the inquisition from a determined interrogator who hails from the shtetl and wants to know, well, everything.

So, before anyone could say "Yosel pisher" (Joe pisspants), Jake had revealed volumes about his origins, family, wife, children, occupation, research interests, salary, house, car, friends, synagogue, rabbi, townsfolk, weather, government, antisemitism, economy, politics ... and where he had bought the suit he was wearing ... and how much it cost! Try keeping things secret when facing men like these. They may look harmless, but ...

Suddenly his jailor interrupted the proceedings: "Where's Rabinovitch?"

Rabinovitch, who never missed a Mincha, had gone missing. So instead of nine Philadelphians in the synagogue, there were only eight! So at that moment Jake was not the tenth man: he was the ninth—and Rabinovitch would be "der tsenter." But he wasn't there!

Their little assembly was now in total disarray: they were still one man short.

"Call the wife," someone offered.

Two-canes went to the phone.

"She says he left half hour ago."

"Let's go look for him. Maybe something happened." This from a truly ancient fellow. And to Jake: "You come too. Maybe you'll see him. You can't miss. He's ninety-two."

Just so he'd know.

The nine of them fanned out over the neighbourhood, Jake in the company of a few creaky hobblers. And did he know how to recognize an ancient Jew named Rabinovitch? Did he know the streets? What if he got lost and couldn't find his way back? Then they'd have only eight. Or nine, if in his absence Rabinovitch was found. But, if so, and he made it back, he'd be "der tsenter" again. He was getting dizzy.

Here he was walking the streets of Philadelphia: "Excuse me, is your name Rabinovitch? … No? Sorry."

Should I ask this guy? "Excuse me, …."

After a few more such attempts, all futile, Jake gave up and found his way back to the synagogue, where he was warmly greeted because in the meantime the other searchers had located Rabinovitch seated on a park bench; he had gotten tired while walking from home. But now Jake was once again, alas, "der tsenter."

Rabinovitch, too, addressed him with: "Fun vanen kumt a Yid?" But, after quickly glancing at his watch, Jake ignored him. Rude, but ….

They prayed. The elders fervently, Jake secularly and nervously, as closing time for the archives was approaching. At last they finished. Jake shook hands all round and was about to take his leave, when two-canes said to him: "OK Canada, now we'll all go over to Mikveh Israel," another synagogue nearby, "because they're probably short of a minyan. And then there's Anshe Chessed, and there's…."

Jake froze. It was coming up to four and he was about to become part of a travelling minyan moving across the city of Philadelphia, synagogue by synagogue. This prayerful perambulation, along with the accompanying interrogations, would keep him there for hours more.

This threat required firmness, so Jake begged off, albeit guiltily.

"Come back again," said two-canes. "We need you." Jake smiled evasively, though he recognized that this was only "pursuing peace," his congregation's declared specialty.

He scooted out the door, raced back to the archives, and got his photocopies just before closing. Then he beetled over to the hotel to pick up his bag and reached the airport just in time to catch his plane—which was delayed for an hour.

So Jake could catch his breath. But just as he had gotten comfortable, sitting in the departure lounge with eyes closed and a warm cup of coffee in his hand, nine bearded men wearing wide fedoras and long black coats walked over to his seat.

Again Jake heard the dreaded words: "Du bist der tsenter."

ENCOUNTER AT DUCK LAKE

It was late afternoon and Jake had finished teaching his class at the Co-op. He had expounded on some of John Kenneth Galbraith's ideas—OK, so he was a socialist idealist. So what?—for the Saskatchewan Farmers' Union branch up in Prince Albert. It was a Saturday in March 1965 and he was driving south on the two-lane highway on his way home to Saskatoon.

Then he spotted him. He was standing beside an old pickup truck, its hood raised and shrouded in smoke.

He slowed down and stopped. He nodded and opened the passenger side door.

"What's up? Can I help?"

"Naw, my rad's shot. You goin down as far as Duck Lake?"

"Yeah, to Saskatoon. Hop in."

Big guy. Swarthy. Coveralls.

"Name's Narcisse."

"Jake."

Silence

"Storm's comin. It'll be a bad one." He was looking out his side window. "You comin from Prince Albert?"

"Yeah."

"What do ya do there?"

"Had a meeting. And you?"

"Had to take my little girl, Louise, to the hospital. Emergency. Stomach pains.

We live near Duck Lake. I'll show you where to let me off. I walk in a mile and a half."

"OK. How old's your girl?"

"Seven and a half. They're gonna keep her for a coupla days. Check her out."

"I hope she's OK."

"Yeah. Thanks. I don't know if you're gonna make it to Saskatoon, buddy. Gonna get dark soon, too."

"Aha."

The sun was getting low, throwing bright streaks across the frozen fields. The snow was getting much thicker, piling up on the hood and between the wiper blades that swished erratically across the windshield. But the car was moving pretty well and Jake could still make out the white highway divider.

Silence

Narcisse looked out the side window and for the next twenty minutes said nothing.

Jake was thinking about next Monday's lecture on the opening of the West.

"Duck Lake, comin up. Six miles. Know what happened near here back in 85?"

"A bit, yeah," Jake said. Wary. He wanted to tell him something.

"A bit? Buddy, you oughta know what really happened here in March of 85. Louis Riel and us breeds started the Northwest rebellion right here with a provisional government because Ottawa and that son of a whore Macdonald wouldn't listen to us. We had grievances: whites stealing our land, kicking our ass, bothering our women, buffalo hunters killing off our herds."

"Mounties bugged us too," he continued." Shot us down, sometimes, the fucken bastards. We took control. And the Mounties tried to put us down. But we kicked the shit out of those fuckers, killed about a dozen of 'em. My gran-gran-père, Narcisse Gravelle, and some of his brothers were there, with their Winchester repeaters. Gran-gran-père was a good shot, could bring down a racing buffalo at two hundred yards. He got two Mounties, one right through the head. They ran, and the Prince Albert whites too. We made 'em run. But they damn near killed our commander, Dumont. And then they hanged Louis Riel. *We'll never forget that.*"

Silence

"Yeah, we made 'em run. The fucken Mounties."

Silence

"Hey, the storm's gettin worse. I get out just down the road a bit. The way it's lookin' you ain't gonna make it to Saskatoon tonight, buddy. Better bunk in at my house for the night. Leave your car on the shoulder and we walk in about mile and a half.

Plows'll go through in the morning. The wife'll make you a good breakfast."

"OK. Thanks. I'll phone home from your house to tell my wife."

"Don't got no phone and the general store's closed by now."

"She'll be worrying. So I'll have to push on, then."

The road was starting to look a little better and the snow was getting lighter. Jake sensed that he could make it home now.

"Up to you, buddy. I get out right here." The village of Duck Lake off to the west a short distance away was a silhouette against the descending sun.

Jake leaned over as he got out. "Listen, thanks for the history lesson. And I hope that your little girl gets better fast."

"Yeah, she'll be OK...."

He smiled. "Her name's Louise Riel Gravelle."

HOW JAKE SAVED CANADA
FROM A RUSSIAN INVASION

United States and British Navy ships often visited Halifax and the summer of 1959 was no exception. Jake was then a Royal Canadian Navy Reserve Lieutenant stationed at HMCS *Shearwater*, the east coast base for the Fleet Air Arm, located near Dartmouth, just across the harbour from Halifax. He served as the Staff Officer for one of the squadrons devoted to anti-submarine detection using Tracker (Grumman-built) two-engined planes loaded with electronic gadgetry and some DC-3s that were less-well equipped. The aircrew were Regular Force RCN Lieutenants and Sub-Lieutenants, except for the squadron's Commanding Officer (CO) and his Executive Officer (XO), both of them Lieutenant Commanders with Second World War service ribbons. The XO's name was Rosenthal, reputedly a superb pilot, and at the first meeting he nodded after seeing the name on the documents Jake presented to him and gave him a look that said "I know that your ethnic origin is the same as mine, but…." He then crisply outlined Jake's duties before ushering him in to meet the CO, who briefly looked at the file, smiled wanly, and uttered words of welcome.

Aircrew, Jake quickly learned, saw themselves as very special people, and woe betide any Reservist assigned to their squadrons at *Shearwater*, or at sea aboard Canada's one and only aircraft carrier, the *Bonaventure* (*Bonny*), who innocently assumed that he was their equal. Jake was one of only two Reserve officers in this squadron, the other one a Lieutenant Commander engineering-type who, Jake learned, was a high school teacher from BC, a quiet pipe-smoker with Second World War ribbons. He took care of technical matters in the hangar, and Jake had no contact with him. From his post in the hangar's main office, Jake was responsible for the squadron's voluminous paper work on personnel and administration. Here he had the assistance of a very able Petty Officer, a twenty-year man who knew everything and told Jake what to do, saving him from numerous mistakes—but not all.

One mistake Jake made early on was to blithely walk into the "crew room" at morning coffee time, plunk his dime into the jar, hail a couple of guys he had met in the Wardroom, and innocently pour himself a cuppa. First came the frozen looks, and Jake wondered if, despite daily showering, he was exuding bad body odour, or if he was unknowingly sporting newly-deposited bird droppings on his uniform. He recoiled. Then came another objection to his presence: they all walked out of the room! Every one of them! Jake thought his teeth must have dropped a foot as he stood there, cup in hand, in a room suddenly empty except for himself. Klutz though he was, he quickly got the point: this was their special turf and Reservists were not—repeat, not—welcome. Jake never entered that sanctum again.

During the ensuing months Jake's relations with many of those guys improved, and a few of them—interestingly, most of them French-Canadians—became fairly friendly in the Wardroom. Others, however, remained prickly, even hostile. One of them, sporting a highly pronounced, though flawed, English accent that Jake spotted as possibly coming from Trinity College at the University of Toronto, where the cultivation of such tones was then in vogue, began chiding him one evening after dinner. Jake was, he claimed, getting a reputation for meeting with the men in his division (the administrative staff), as was his duty according to the manual he received, and urging some of them to get more education, like finishing high school, to improve their chances of advancing up the ranks in the Navy. "You are showing the rest of us up!" he roared, his fourth gin and tonic slopping over his hand. He said that he was going to challenge Jake to a fistfight outside. Although only five foot six and a mere a hundred and forty pounds, Jake had had some success by following the advice of "Boyo" Evans, the boxing coach at his hometown YMCA, who had counseled: "Always go for the nose, boyo, the nose!" So Jake just smiled and nodded assent, and he of the fake accent balked, then wandered off.

There was also some antisemitism. On one occasion in the Wardroom, a senior officer, a Commander, who had had a few before dinner, a propos of nothing said to Jake: "You know, Tabsky, we're not in this man's Navy for our *personal profit!*"

"What do you mean by that, Sir, and my name is Tabachnik, Sir."

"Well, I know a lot of you Jews and … I come from the North End of Winnipeg and…."

"Sir—"

They were interrupted by another senior officer who had hastened to the scene and was nervously whispering into the three-striper's ear. Jake left the table.

Drinking parties went on often, especially on weekends, and Jake was invited to a few of those. They were usually held at the apartments (near the base) of married officers. Wives and girl-friends were usually in attendance. He brought along his twelve-pack, a mickey, or bottle of wine, of course, and blathered the evening away like the rest of them. At this time he had neither wife nor girlfriend, and though he had met a few women in Halifax, there was no easy way to bring them over to *Shearwater* (he had no car); and in any case, he didn't think that they would be comfortable in this environment, which sometimes got raucous.

One flyer was going off to the *Bonny* for a spell and kindly loaned Jake his car, a lovely new white Pontiac convertible, allowing him to drive it where he wished. He did so for a couple of days after duty hours and really enjoyed getting around Bedford Basin, the enormous inland sea back of Halifax, where convoys had assembled during the Second World War before crossing the Atlantic to Britain. Then three well-lubricated, self-proclaimed buddies of Pontiac man confronted Jake menacingly at one of these parties, demanding on his supposed behalf the keys to the car. Three! Three against a twerp like Jake! So, instead of telling them to go stuff themselves, thereby having to duke it out with all of them simultaneously, Jake surrendered the keys with a smile—telling them, truthfully, that the gas tank was just about bone dry anyway, and that they'd likely have to push the car to the nearest gas station.

Guess he won that one all right. Don't mess with a Reservist.

But the apogee of Jake's experience with Regular Force/Reservist tension occurred when he inadvertently put his foot in it with the Squadron CO. This happened when a small part of the huge United States Navy's Atlantic Fleet arrived one day with about a dozen destroyers and minesweepers, a very large supply ship, and a mid-sized aircraft carrier. There were also many hundreds of officers and enlisted men thirsting for alcoholic refreshment that was strictly forbidden them aboard ship. The sailors flooded into the harbourfront and Barrington and Gottingen Street taverns, speakeasys, blind pigs, and other "establishments," while the streets were monitored by groups of Shore Patrol United States Marines armed with batons and pistols picking up strays. During these hours American Navy officers, dozens of them, crowded into our Wardroom, imbibing and carousing long, long into the night. Many of *Shearwater*'s senior officers joined them in happy hands-across-the-border spirit of conviviality, which was generously paid for by the Americans. The RCN officers included Jake's CO who, he had been informed by his Petty Officer, knew right well how to tie one on.

But—and this is a big one—early next morning at 0800 hours, just after Jake got to his desk, entirely sober because he had not attended the previous evening's event, a sealed envelope marked TOP SECRET was delivered to the Squadron office.

"Holy shit, what do I do now?" he thought.

Gevalt. Gott zoll uphiten.

"Sir, you've got to take this to the CO right now," said his Petty Officer, who could see distress across Jake's face.

"Yeah, PO, but he's not here." The time was now 0810.

"Then the Executive Officer, sir."

"Rosenthal's not here either. On leave."

"You can't wait any longer, sir."

Silence.

"Where does the CO live?"

"Nearby, sir. I know where."

"Let's get there now."

He scrounged a vehicle and drove Jake to the CO's house. He pounded on the door. It was now 0820.

After about three minutes a woman in nightdress came angrily to the door.

"What the hell do you want?"

"I need to see the Lieutenant Commander right now. I'm Lieutenant Tabachnik, Squadron Staff Officer."

"Why?"

"It's urgent. I need to see him *right now*, ma'am."

"Oh shit. What did you say your name is?"

"It's urgent, ma'am. *It's urgent.*"

"Wait here."

"This is urgent, ma'am! Please get him here now!"

"Mouthy little bugger, arnchya." She slammed the door.

Minutes passed. Where the hell was he?

Eyes like two piss holes in the snow bedecked the bloated face that next appeared.

"Whad iz dhis, Tabski?"

"Sir, this message arrived at the squadron office at 0800 hours." Jake handed him the envelope.

He scratched it open. Read it. He gasped.

"Waid 'ere." He went inside. In five minutes he appeared in uniform holding a cup of strong-smelling coffee, his face solemn and his eyes alert. Remarkable!

"Let's go," he barked.

They raced back to the Squadron where the CO got two fully-manned Trackers out on the tarmac fuelled up and aloft within about ten minutes. Two more were being prepared.

Why? What did the TOP SECRET message contain?

Jake soon found out that it was an order from Atlantic Command to get Trackers in the air immediately because of a reported sighting of what was believed to be a Russian submarine cruising in Canadian waters just off Lunenburg. Shadowing the American fleet??

So, by 840 the Royal Canadian Navy's Fleet Air Arm was out on patrol. And sure enough, some fifty miles offshore, the guys sighted the mysterious sub, then steaming east, whose officers saw them coming and ordered a crash-dive before a possible identification.

So doesn't Jake deserve a medal for saving Canada?

After all, if it weren't for him, a mere Reserve Lieutenant, and his Petty Officer assistant, maybe we'd all be speaking Russian.

GLOSSARY

Below are brief definitions of the Yiddish and Hebrew terms found in this book. Many explanations could have been much longer, as a number of terms carry complex cultural and/or religious meanings. But the purpose of this glossary is simply to elucidate, in as basic a manner as possible, those words and expressions that might be unfamiliar to non-Jewish readers.

Bested: bastard
Bidny chlopchik: poor boy
Bima: pulpit from which the Torah is read
Blady: filthy whore
Chazerim: pigs
Cheder: afternoon religious school
Choleri: carrier of cholera
Chutzpah: cheek, nerve
Curveh: prostitute
Farkakte: befouled (literally: "shitty")
Ganovim: thieves
Golden Horde: Genghis Khan
Haftorah: special section of the Torah
Irgun: resistance organization in British Mandate Palestine
Kibbutznik: member of a kibbutz, an Israeli collective settlement
Kiddush: wine, whiskey and munchies consumed after services
Kol Nidre: opening prayer on Yom Kippur, the Day of Atonement

Kosher: ritually approved
Maccabees: warrior kings of ancient Israel known for their
brutality
Mamzerim: bastards
Maven: knowledgeable person, self-styled expert
Mincha: daily afternoon prayers
Minyan: quorum (of ten men) for prayer
Nudnik: bothersome individual
Oisvorf: worthless individual
Oy, Gott zol Uphiten: may God look down
Paskudnik: troublesome youth
Shabbos: Sabbath
Shamess: synagogue caretaker
Schecht: ritual slaughter of animals for human consumption
Schnorrer: social parasite
Shmendrick: awkward individual
Shidduch: introduction (most likely leading to a wedding)
Shlemiel: socially inept individual
Shtarker: strong man, tough guy (as in brave and courageous)
Shtetl: small town or community
Shtick: personal gimmick, usually comic
Shul: synagogue
Tallit: prayer shawl
Yiddishn Gass: the Jewish "street" (where Jews gather)
Yiddishkeit: Jewish culture
Zindele mein: my sonny boy
Zolln zai brennen: may they burn in Hell

Lightning Source UK Ltd.
Milton Keynes UK
UKOW03f1512300117
293183UK00002B/493/P